WITCH CATASTROPHE IN WESTERHAM

Paranormal Investigation Bureau Book 17

DIONNE LISTER

Dionne Lister

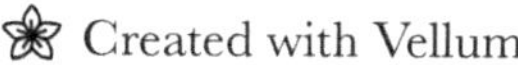 Created with Vellum

CHAPTER 1

"Wow, the place is gor—" I stopped just inside the doorway, the sight in the living room beyond halting both my words and my feet.

Angelica, who'd been leading the way, ceased walking and turned back to me. "What's wrong, dear?"

"I was going to say how gorgeous the place was, but that cage kind of wrecks it." A steel-barred cage sat the middle of the large room, ruining the elegant effect of timber floors, crisp white walls, and gothic-style stone-framed windows in Angelica's Cotswold cottage. Thick curtains hung over the windows. Definitely a precaution against people seeing the monstrosity inside. And I was talking about Chad, not the cage. "I have to say, I'm disappointed to be finding out about your holiday house so late in the game."

Angelica shrugged one shoulder. "Sorry, dear. I try to keep this place a secret. No one other than James and your mother knows about this place."

"Now I know, and so does that idiot." Chad glared at me

from his seat in one corner of the cage. It was big enough for an armchair—how thoughtful of Angelica—and a single bed.

"Yes, but neither of you knows the address or coordinates. And he doesn't even know this is mine, or that it's in the Cotswolds." Angelica had put up a total bubble of silence when we'd stepped into the reception room. "Don't tell him anything."

"Witch's honour, I won't say anything."

She raised a brow. "Witch's honour? What nonsense are you going on about now?"

"Would you rather that I swore on my mother's life?"

"Don't be ridiculous, Lily. Just saying okay would be sufficient."

"Okay. Okay."

"Once is enough."

"Okay." I smirked. The two okays were for different things, but it was kind of amusing, and the third one sealed the deal.

She shook her head. "Let's hurry along, dear. He has a message to call Brosnan back. I could spell him to say what we want, but it's complicated. There's a margin for error. It would be easier if he had incentive."

"Okay." She folded her arms and gave me a *look.* "Ah, no, I didn't mean it as a joke. I'm agreeing with you. You did say that a simple okay would suffice, did you not?"

She sighed. "I suppose I did. Just hurry it along. I'm going to drop the bubble of total silence now." Not wanting to poke the bear any more than I already had, I kept my okay to myself and just nodded.

Angelica dropped the spell, and we made our way to the cage. Chad glared up at us, a silver bracelet gleaming from his wrist. Angelica had kept hold of the one that Beren's brother had used on me last week. They'd also found two more at the house he'd rented for the *wedding*. I shuddered. That had been a close call for Liv and me. But we were all fine, so time to move on. James was holding onto one of the bracelets, and Millicent's dad was studying the other with a view to creating improved magic-blocking implements. The bracelets had a different set-up to the PIB handcuffs, apparently. Not that that meant much to me. Technically, I had as much insight into magic as I did into the way a plane worked. I just used it and trusted the process. Sometimes I crashed and burned, and sometimes I reached my destination.

Chad stood and folded his arms. "Let me out of here. This is pee-posterous!"

I laughed. "Is that 'pee' as in the little, green, round things or the wet, yellow stuff?" Angelica's lips twitched, but she held her mirth inside like a good agent. Chad just looked blankly. I shook my head. He really had no idea how stupid he was.

He pressed his lips together and pointed at Angelica, then me. "You're both going to spend the rest of your lives in jail for this… arresting the acting head of the PIB. I've never heard of anything so disgusting. Traitors!"

Angelica managed a surprised expression. "Oh, reeeeally, Chad. Is that before or after the directors kill us?" She made a good point. That's what he'd said would happen when the directors found out we'd discovered their secret to shut everything down to help a huge criminal organisation. How much money were they getting for that? If they were paying the idiot in the cage two million pounds, they must be making a fortune.

He answered with a harrumph. That was probably the smartest thing he'd ever said… or sounded out.

Angelica looked at me and gave a slight chin tip. That was the signal for me to go for it. We needed leverage with him so he'd do what we wanted. As much as we were in this neck-deep, Angelica and James wanted to maintain some semblance of respect for the law and PIB rules. So, instead of controlling his mind—which was highly illegal and took a lot of skill and energy—they wanted to use old-fashioned blackmail. An audio device was always listening and would record everything to a computer at James's place. It was time for me to do what I came for.

Chad couldn't lie to me, and it tickled my little heart every time his face smooshed with frustration after he'd said something he hadn't wanted to. According to James and Angelica, this wasn't breaking the rules since he'd accidentally cast the must-answer-and-answer-truthfully spell on himself.

I rubbed my hands together and grinned. Angelica looked at me and raised a brow. "You're enjoying this entirely too much."

"Really? You really think that?"

She tapped her chin several times in thought. "Okay, maybe not. You have me there. But I should exude some semblance of sensibleness."

"Fair enough. Being in charge does have its downside."

She gave me a grave look. "It certainly does, dear. It certainly does."

Chad fell back into his armchair. His legs lifted, as if he was going to plonk them on a table, but there was no table, and they fell to the floor with a thump. He scowled. Angelica and I both smiled. Sucked in, Chadiot.

I magicked an armchair from across the room and sat. I folded my hands in my lap. "So, Chaddy, I'm going to ask you a few questions."

His eyes widened. "No!"

"You would be doing the exact same thing to me, had your spell worked. All I can say is bad luck. Suck it up."

He jumped to his feet. Looking at Angelica, he pointed at me. "Are you just going to let her talk to me like that? This is a level of disrespect I've never seen at the PIB."

Angelica's gaze turned flinty, her tone cold. "I've seen that level of disrespect before. When a certain someone named Chad blah, blah, blah the third took over my job. Now that the shoe is on the other foot, I hope it gives you blisters." Ooh, Angelica didn't usually let people get to her, but then again, because of Chad and the directors, she'd had to leave the PIB and take crap from Chad, a clearly inferior being of questionable intelligence. It had to hurt every time she'd dealt with him before we'd taken matters way over the line. I'd seen her bite her tongue on so many occasions that this was probably a smidgeon of the vitriol she should be dishing out.

Chad sat up straighter. He inhaled violently, his chest puffing up in indignation. His mouth opened, and I held up my hand. He didn't get to defend himself anymore. It was time for more answers. "What's your favourite ice cream flavour?" Oh my God, *that* was the first question that came to my brain? I shook my head at myself.

Whatever complaint had manifested in his mouth, it disappeared, replaced by, "Octopus."

What the…? How was that even an ice cream flavour? I squeezed my eyes shut for a moment. Ew. If it hadn't been for the spell, I would've thought he was lying. Maybe he'd misheard me? Could magic do that, make a mistake? I opened my eyes. "Your favourite *ice cream*"—I made sure to enunciate it clearly—"is octopus?"

He lifted his chin and folded his arms. "Yes. So what?"

Angelica and I shared a disturbed look; then I turned back

to him again. "It's just gross. That's all." I cleared my throat. Time for questions we could use the answers to. Angelica had briefed me last night about what she wanted asked. I just needed to pick one and go with it. "Are there plans to shut down any other PIB offices?"

"Yes. New York." He slapped his hand over his mouth way too late. I smirked. Not that the answer made me happy, but his discomfort was such a joy to behold.

"Do all the UK directors know what's going on."

"Yes."

I turned to Angelica, finding only her poker face. She was giving me nothing, which likely meant bad things. The head director had been on her side, as far as we'd all thought. Were we wrong, or was he pretending to be in on it so he could foil it later? He'd obviously never said anything to Angelica, because this shutting-down-the-PIB thing had come as a huge shock to her. It did mean that we couldn't approach him now or ask for his help, just in case. So typical that things had to become more complicated. It was a theme in my life.

"Do the New York directors know anything about it?"

"One of four."

"What's his name?"

"Ronald Reagan."

Of course it was. I looked at Angelica. "Do they do western-movie actors over there, or is this a president thing?"

"A president thing, dear. They're very patriotic."

"Okay. I suppose presidents are just as good a choice as *James Bond* actors." I hooked my gaze on Chad. He squirmed and turned slightly away from me. Something on the ground suddenly seized his interest. *You can't run, and you can't hide, Chadiot.* Next question coming up. "When is your next face-to-face meeting with the directors, and where is it?"

"Tomorrow, 7:00 p.m. at the London office in Mayfair." He slammed a fist down onto the chair arm.

"Sucks to be you right now, doesn't it?"

He glared and gritted out, "Yes."

I chuckled. He hadn't wanted to agree, but the spell demanded he be truthful. This was too much fun. "What were you supposed to do when the UK PIB shut down and you returned to New York?"

His lips pressed together, then tried to open. Sweat popped out on his forehead as he attempted to resist, and his lips performed a bizarre wriggle-undulation combo like lizard tails that had just fallen off. "I— w— was to start the ball rolling over there so we could eventually shut it down." His breath sawed in and out as if he'd just sprinted a few laps around the living room. Telling the truth could be hard work.

"When were you planning on firing Will?"

"Next week."

"Was anyone else supposed to be fired at the same time?"

"Yes. Imani." His chin tipped up at this, defiance in his eyes. Of course he would gloat over that.

"Do you still think that's going to happen?"

"Yes, probably. I'm going to get out of here and tell the directors. When they find out, you'll all be as good as dead. I may not get to fire any of you if they get to you first though. That's the only negative in this whole darn situation. I wanted to see you all suffer first."

I rolled my eyes. What a charming man. "Do you have to do what we say?" This was to confirm what Angelica thought from the look of the spell—it wasn't just to tell the truth; it could also be used to order people around. He'd told me to find out what I could about Angelica and had assumed I would comply, but it was better to be safe than sorry. Who knew—he might have just thought I was scared of him and would obey out of fear. Never going to happen.

His face twisted with the effort of keeping his mouth shut. He lost. "Yes." Tears flooded his eyes and rolled down his reddened cheeks. Poor baby.

I believed him, but best to test our theory before we sent him into the lion's den tomorrow. I drew on my magic, and a small plastic container appeared in my hand. It was empty, but it wouldn't be for long. I pictured Angelica's backyard and willed something into the container. Six small, dark pellets appeared. Even I could admit I was terribly cruel as I magicked the container into his lap. "Eat what's in the container."

Angelica's eyes widened. "You're not…."

I looked at her. "We need to know if he'll do exactly as we say. If it's too easy, it won't work. Our lives depend on it."

She blew out a breath. "Fine. You're right." That admission likely pained her. If only we didn't have to be in this situation in the first place.

Chad sobbed. "Is this rat poo?"

I made a game-show-fail noise. "Ba bow. Guess again!"

His brow furrowed, and his bottom lip quivered. "Squirrel poo?"

I nodded, a sage expression on my face. "We have a winner, folks! I'd like you to eat all the squirrel poo, please. It's not that much. Just be thankful I don't own a dog." I tapped my chin with my index finger. "Oh, that's right. I do! And home's only a portal away." I grinned. Another reason I was going to hell. Oh, well. Might as well do the crime if I was going to do the time.

Chad's mouth stayed closed, but his brows drew together, as if they were trying to touch and give each other comfort.

His hand gripped the container. He stared into it, haunted. At least I'd picked something he found horrific—he didn't strike me as a good actor.

I leaned forward. "Eat. The. Poo." I smiled. It wasn't every day I got to say that. Shame Will and Imani weren't here to watch this. They would've enjoyed it. I didn't want to film it because that was just too cruel. Or was it?

His shaking hands lifted the container to his mouth, which slowly opened. He tilted his head back, squeezed his eyes shut, and tipped the little brown pellets into his mouth. I would've magicked the poo away, but he had to know we would be true to our word. If we threatened him, he had to know we'd go through with it, no matter what. Because I wasn't the most horrible person on the planet, I magicked a glass of water onto the small side table next to his armchair. "There's water there if you want to wash out the taste."

His eyes sprang open. He grabbed the water and threw it down his throat, then looked up at me, and I almost apologised. Defeat and fear swam in his gaze, but anger nipped at their tails, reminding me of all the crap things he'd done to me and those I loved, all for money. He had no scruples—he was happy to have a lawless society, at least when it came to witches, and he was ready to stand by and watch us all get murdered. Grrr. My jaw clenched. *That stinking pile of sh—*

Angelica touched my arm. "Lily, are you all right?"

I shook myself out of my escalating rage spiral and met her gaze. "Yes, thanks, Ma'am. I'm extremely all right." I hoped Chad took notice of the fact I'd called her Ma'am. She was in charge again, and God, it felt good. Even if it wasn't a sanctioned change, it was legit as far as I was concerned.

She assessed me for a moment longer, then looked at

Chad. "Lily has something else to tell you, so you'd better listen up."

He sneered but wisely kept quiet.

I folded my arms and gave him my best "you're going to do what I say or else" glare. "Tomorrow, when you go to that meeting, you are going to act as if nothing has happened. You are going to pretend all is well at the **PIB** and with the directors' plans, and if they ask you about Angelica, James, Will, Imani, Liv, Millicent, or Beren, you are going to tell them they've been working hard and you're going to fire Will and Imani next week. If they ask about me, you're going to tell them my special talents include truth-telling—just like my brother—and heightened observation. When you are finished with the meeting, you are going to magic yourself back to **PIB** headquarters, go to your office, and wait there for Angelica. Before you go, Angelica will take off that bracelet, but you will not draw power to go against my wishes. You will not draw power to go against any **PIB** agent or me. You will not draw power to undo the spell that you cast and which you now wear. When you are with the directors, you will only think thoughts that everything is going well." Just in case they demanded to read his mind, we needed to have all our bases covered. Hopefully none of them would think to check his aura for spells. There wasn't anything we could do about that, and if we sent him in with the bracelet on, they'd sense he couldn't use his magic. I scratched the side of my nose. Was that everything?

"I think that's it, dear."

My spine itched. It was still too risky. "Is there a masking spell we can use to hide that other spell?"

Angelica made a total bubble of silence. "We could possibly try, but the masking spell would leave its mark and look even more suspicious."

I glanced at Chad and wrinkled my forehead. "It's still too much of a gamble. Surely the directors will notice it."

She rubbed her forehead—a rare show of frustration. "I agree. I was hoping to come up with something myself, but we might as well nut this out now."

"Could we get Lavender to cast an illusion on the spell, make it look like something harmless, like he's wearing a spell to make him look better to non-witches?"

"Possibly. It's not easy though. How good is Lavender?"

"I think he's one of the best. He's managed exceptional illusion spells that have fooled non-witches."

"Yes, but witches?"

I sighed. "I don't know." Back to square one. Why was foiling witch criminals so hard?

"Leave it with me, dear. I'll have a chat to Millicent's father this afternoon."

"Okay." I didn't want to point out that he'd have less than twenty-four hours to come up with something—Angelica already knew. We could've ignored the whole aura thing—it would've been easier—but it was a glaring weak spot in our plan. I was betting that Angelica had decided to figure it out by herself, but it was better mentioning it rather than being sorry later. "What if we can't solve it?"

"We may have to get him to cancel the meeting, but I doubt that will do more than put it off for a day, and we don't want them to get suspicious. I would doubt he's ever cancelled a meeting with them before. They picked him because he's subservient. He's a weak, greedy brown-noser." She gave me an encouraging smile. "Don't worry, dear. We'll find a way. We always do."

But had we always found a way? Yes, we'd come this far, but there were still so many obstacles to navigate. It seemed as if we just swapped one frying pan for another, and each pan was successively hotter. Pretty soon, we were going to run out of frying pans and land in the proverbial fire. Burning to a crisp was not the way I wanted to leave this earth.

It would be nice to have choices for once. Was that too much to ask?

CHAPTER 2

After the morning dramas, I was ready for some relaxation time. Who knew how much longer I'd be able to roam about in the wild? If the directors realised what was going on, it would be back to holing up at home. Argh. My plan was to have a wander around the Natural History Museum in London. I texted Lavender to see what he was up to because as well as enjoying his company, I wanted to sus out his spell-camouflaging skills.

Within a minute of texting him, my phone rang. "Hey, Lav! What say you?"

"I say yes! Is it okay if Sarah comes with?"

"Sounds good to me. The more, the merrier."

And that's how it was that I walked out of the public toilets just ahead of Sarah to find Lavender already waiting in the grand entry foyer of the museum. Even on a weekday, lots of people milled around, their voices echoing off the tiled floor and stone walls to float up into the cavernous ceiling above. I eyed the sign that pointed the way to food. Sarah laughed.

"Trust you. Let's check out the ground floor first; then we'll go eat."

I looked at Lavender. "Whose bright idea was it to bring her?"

Lavender laughed. "All mine, darling. Just to make up for it, lunch is on me… when we finally get it. Do you think you can keep the beast quiet until then?" His gaze moved to my stomach.

"I'll try, but I can't guarantee anything."

Sarah grinned and pulled me into a hug. "So good to see you, almost-sister-in-law. When are you guys tying the knot anyway? I want some nieces and nephews to spoil."

My eyes widened. "Oh, God. Not yet. Let me enjoy my life a little bit more before it all comes to an end."

Lavender chuckled. "I hear you, sister. Once the kids come along, no more sleep-ins, no more all-night parties." He waggled his brows at Sarah. "Maybe you should have some of your own rather than bother Lily about it."

She shook her head rather vigorously. "No. Way." She linked her arm with mine and pulled me along. "Let's explore this place."

Lavender fell into step on my other side and entwined his arm with my free one. "Funny how she's suddenly keen to get going, even though she's probably been here about five times."

Sarah shrugged. "So what? There's always something to learn."

Lavender and I smirked at each other. At least I'd gotten her off the topic of me birthing offspring. It wasn't that I never wanted kids. It was something to ponder way, way, way into the future… that was, if I even had a future. And did I want to put children through what James and I had been through? What if Will and I had kids, and then someone killed us?

"Lily? Hello, are you there?" Sarah waved her hand in front of my face.

"Oops, sorry." I smiled. "Ooh, look, dinosaur bones." Even though I wanted to chat to Lavender about his talent, I still wanted to enjoy our outing. Who knew, it might be my last? *So dramatic, Lily.*

"Big and old too." Sarah grinned. "So, what's prompted this get-together?"

I cast a garble spell around us. I didn't feel like letting people hear the word "witch" and staring at me like I was nuts. "I wanted to ask our esteemed lavender-haired friend about his talent at camouflaging spells in auras from other witches. I'm not even sure if you can, but I know you're good with using magic to make people look very different. I get that it's always to fool non-witches, but do you think you could make a spell symbol on someone's aura look different or even hide it?"

Lavender stopped abruptly in front of a large dinosaur skeleton that was mounted on the wall, under glass. A woman pushing a stroller took quick evasive action and pivoted around us. Lavender cocked his head to the side. "I would say no, but I've never actually tried."

"Do you think it's possible?" I crossed my fingers on both hands.

"Hmm…. Maybe? Is this urgent?"

I cast an absolute bubble of silence. This was just too important. "Yes. Chad's going to a meeting with the directors tomorrow. We know he has to do what we say, but we're worried they'll notice the spell in his aura." Will had filled Sarah in the day it happened, just in case we needed help from the French bureau in the coming days. She hadn't told the head agent at the French office yet—we were saving that as a last resort.

Sarah looked at Lavender. "Why don't we spend fifteen more minutes having a quick look around this level; then we'll grab lunch and head over to Lily's?"

"You wouldn't mind?" I asked. I didn't want to make them do boring stuff on their day off.

Lavender grinned. "Not at all. It's a good excuse to experiment. And you know I love experimenting." He winked.

I laughed and took in his bright-yellow T-shirt, lime-green, knee-length jean shorts, and his platform black-and-white sneakers. "Yes, we do know. Okay. So, let's pretend we're just here for the exhibits for the next fifteen minutes. I'm going to drop the BOTS." They both nodded, and I cut off my magic. I slid my arms out of theirs and pulled my phone out of my pocket. "I might as well take some photos while I'm here—use them as a reference for next time. Maybe I'll get to see the whole place in the future, if I'm still alive."

Sarah gasped and slapped my arm. "Lily! Don't say that. I bet we'll be around to celebrate our eightieth birthdays together. No depressing talk."

"Fine. Whatever you say." I deserved that rebuke, but I wasn't going to apologise for being a realist. Sometimes my positivity and realism were at odds. Or maybe being positive just helped me get through to the point where everything worked out. I was good at pushing through even if I didn't think I'd survive. What else could anyone do? Giving up, no matter how dismal things looked, was never an option.

"Can we double back to the entry? It was such a gorgeous space. I want to get a couple of pics there first."

"Of course." Lavender turned and led the way past the dinosaurs and into the vast foyer that was as grand as a church with stained-glass windows and stone archways. I craned my neck to look up at the ceiling that must have floated three or four stories above us. Light cascaded into the space from glass panels that made up part of the ceiling. Two imposing staircases bled people into the area—one staircase at each end of the main hall. I walked to one end, so I could get most of the space into my shot, Lavender and Sarah trailing behind me.

I held my phone up in landscape mode and clicked. Then I took a couple in portrait mode, centring the churchlike windows at the other end. The hairs on my nape stood on end. I shivered and pushed down the rising nausea. I lowered my camera. This couldn't be right. I licked my lips and brought up the photos. "Can you guys look at these photos and tell me what you see?" I tilted the phone towards them.

"That woman's taste in clothing is appalling," Lavender said as he pointed to one of the women in the shot. I would've laughed, but something was seriously wrong.

Sarah sucked in a breath. "Oh. Oh my God." She looked up from the photo and across the hall, then back down to the photo again. "Really look, Lav."

His hand slammed over his mouth. "No way."

I swallowed. "Yes way."

"Take another photo." Sarah stared at me, her expression one of hopeless hope—and, yes, that's the expression you have when you know something's true, but you don't want to believe it.

I held my phone up and clicked again. Not much had changed. A few people had left the hall, and a few new people had entered. "It's consistent with the last pic. Those five people"—I touched the screen in three places to single them out—"are still see through. Two of the other see-through people left the hall, and there's one more who's just come in the front door."

Sarah said, "Two of them work here, and the others are all in business attire."

Lavender nodded. "It's twelve thirty-five. I suppose people like to come here during their lunch hour."

I shook my head. "But why are so many of them going to die? And they're mostly young people. This guy here looks like he's in his fifties, but the rest are twenties and thirties. So it's probably not an illness." I'd never taken a photo that showed multiple people dying. The horror of it wasn't fully formed inside me. I was probably still adjusting to the reality of it. What the hell was going to happen?

Sarah looked around at the people wandering about. "Maybe it's just a freaky thing… a coincidence?"

"What if something's going to happen here today?" That would make sense. My heart picked up tempo. "Maybe we should get out of here?"

Lavender looked at me. "We can't just run away. We have to try and stop whatever it is from happening."

"Lav's right." Sarah touched my forearm. "Take a photo of the both of us. If we're see through, we'll leave, and if we're not, we'll stay and try and get to the bottom of it."

"That makes sense. Maybe I'll take a selfie."

Lavender's eyes widened. "Can you see your own demise? Why would you want to?"

"I have no idea. And for the same reason as you—if I'm going to die because I'm here, best I get the hell out. If that does happen, we'll go to Angelica's and take another photo, make sure we did the right thing." Foretelling my own death wasn't on my top ten list of things I'd love to do, but fore-warned was forearmed as they said.

Lavender laughed. "Yeah, that would be hilarious if we only died because we went there."

Sarah rolled her eyes. "Yes, super hilarious."

I took a deep breath and ignored the way my stomach lurched. "Let's get this over and done with. Get in close." They huddled up next to me, one on either side. Their warmth wasn't enough to banish the chill cascading over me. I pressed the icon that turned the camera to face us, held up my phone, and said, "Cheese." I managed a smile as I clicked because we hadn't appeared see through on the screen. The photo confirmed it.

Lavender let out a huge breath. "We're going to live!"

I grinned. "Yes, we are. So maybe whatever it is doesn't happen today?"

Sarah tucked a strand of hair behind her ear. "Or doesn't happen while we're here. We're going home after lunch."

As much as I wanted to eat, that gave us time to investigate. We could always go to Costa afterwards. Chocolate muffins and coffee were good any time of day. "Okay. I'm going to keep taking photos, see if we can identify any kind of pattern. And I want to go outside and photograph as much as possible. What if whatever it is doesn't happen here specifically?" I swallowed the lump of vomit that wanted to ascend. "What if it's more widespread?"

Sarah shook her head. "Please don't say that."

Lavender lowered his voice because none of us had had the good sense to make a bubble of silence—bad things happened when shock took over. "Are you thinking a terrorist attack?"

I made a bubble of silence. No reason we should give all our secrets away. Hopefully no one had been listening in to our conversation about the photographs. It was unlikely since all our phones were magically protected against eavesdropping, but you never knew. "Possibly. Or some kind of natural disaster that collapses buildings. If I can narrow down the area, we'll have more of an idea."

"We should probably call my brother, see if the PIB has any intelligence that might shed some light on this."

"I don't want to jeopardise people's lives, but if Will finds out, he'll make sure we get out of here. I need to take more photos."

"I can tell him that we're not see through."

Lavender pursed his lips, then said, "I don't know, Sar. I think Lily's right. Just give her ten minutes to have a better look around. We all know what Will's like, especially when it comes to protecting you two."

She sighed. There was no arguing with Lavender's assessment. "Okay, then." She pulled her phone out and looked at the time. "Ten minutes, starting now."

"Done." I gave a nod, started filming, then hurried outside. If I didn't find anything, I'd race back inside and pin down the locations where people were see through. I turned right and walked with my video on. That worked just as well as looking through the camera setting. I scanned left to right, making sure I got everyone across the busy road and on my own side. I walked in one direction for a minute, every fifth or sixth person showing up see through. This was damned scary.

I kept walking.

The further I walked, the fewer the people who were see through, but even after five minutes, there was still the odd person who was going to die. Whether that was from whatever was going to happen or not, I couldn't say. How many of the people who had shown up see through were going to die by natural causes rather than this event? I'd never taken a crowd sample before, but I was sure I'd remember if lots of people had turned up see through before. It was usually pretty rare, not that I ran around taking photos of crowds, and I wasn't about to start. Knowing someone was going to die was a horrible thing to experience. The less I went through that, the better.

I turned around and headed back towards the museum, videoing as I went. When I reached the museum, I kept walking, determined to figure this out, no matter how confronting it was. I turned left at the tube station on the corner. A man in office attire, earbuds in and laptop bag in hand, hurried towards me. His ghostly image in my screen sending a shudder through me. I turned and followed him—and that didn't look weird, videoing a stranger. Stalker much? I quickly cast a no-notice spell on myself.

He headed down the stairs to the South Kensington Tube station. I followed.

Our footsteps echoed in the tunnel but were barely audible above the chaotic organ music bouncing off the brick walls. Who knew organs were so annoying? The guy playing was just up ahead, sitting on a stool, the battery-operated keyboard on his lap. Sorry, buddy, but I wasn't going to throw a coin on your jacket.

Excited voices reverberated through the tunnel, announcing a group of teenage girls coming towards me, excitedly talking about a cute guy one of them was dating—none of them were see through. I blew out a relieved breath. Old people, two at a time or singly, ambled through, some with walking sticks, some without. Only one of them was see through. That didn't tell me much.

A man and woman, both wearing white shirts and black jeans, maybe in their forties, came my way, both of them see through. Was that a uniform for a bar or restaurant? At least I was recording all this, and we could all pick it apart later.

My phone rang, and I started, almost dropping it. *Damn it!* I stopped filming and answered it. "Hey, Sarah."

"Hey, Lily. Will said to get home ASAP."

"Of course he did, but he's not the boss of me, so…."

She chuckled. "Me neither. How long till you come back?"

"At least five minutes, maybe ten. I have a lead. I'll see you soon."

"Bye."

"Bye."

I put the ringer on silent—in case Will decided to bother me and demand I go home—and started filming again.

We finally reached the ticket barriers, but I didn't have a card or ticket to enter. I filmed the guy going through the gates. Six others walking around the area were see through, but that was it. Still, I was pretty sure that was more than was statistically normal. In total today, I'd counted about forty-seven "ghosts." A couple or maybe up to five might have been going to die anyway, but I couldn't believe that thirty-seven people from such a small sample were all going to die in different, non-suspicious ways.

I turned around and headed back. Disappointment shadowed me—we were no closer to figuring this out than before. I filmed the whole way back, catching a few more ghostly images, which proved that whatever was going to kill these people was still happening.

How long did we have? An hour, a day, a week? One thing I did actually know—we didn't have long to solve this.

A disaster was coming, and the likelihood of us preventing it was slim.

I refused to believe it was none.

CHAPTER 3

I rejoined Lav and Sarah at the museum; then we travelled back via the toilet cubicles. We sat on one of Angelica's Chesterfields, the three of us sticking together for support, me in between them. Will stood in front of the Chesterfield opposite, hands on hips, glaring down at us. James stood next to him nodding as Will spoke. "What were you thinking, not telling us straight away? I can't believe you didn't just get out of there. You should all know better."

I folded my arms. "Look, Mr Bossy Boots Crankypants, Lavender and Sarah are agents in training, and, according to you and James, I'm one of the most powerful witches around. I want you to also note that we were not see through in the photo. Stop being an overprotective annoyance."

His eyes widened, and he took a deep breath. "Wha—"

Sarah stood and looked him in the eye. "Just be careful what you say, big brother. I know you worry, but we weren't in any danger. We can do without all this drama. In case you missed the major point, a huge catastrophe is coming, and we need to try and stop it. Now keep your mouth shut and watch the videos Lily took. There's also a few photos." She turned to me and held her hand out. I magicked my phone into it with the photo app open.

Will gave her a dirty look but took the phone in a civilised manner. He and James sat just as Angelica entered the room. "What have I missed?"

James turned his head to look at her as she made her way to the Chesterfield and sat next to Will. "We were just about to watch a video that Lily took today at the Natural History Museum." Will pressed Play, and as they watched the videos, James relayed what we'd told them.

When they were done, James's magic tingled my scalp, and a video screen hovered in the air in the middle of the room. He said, "Play the videos Lily took, one after the other."

A huge image of the museum's ginormous hall appeared on the screen. Eight, then nine see-through people appeared before the shot moved outside. After a minute, James said, "Pause video." He'd stopped it as I'd filmed from my side of the street across to the other. "Do you notice something?"

Angelica's brow wrinkled. "Hmm, yes. Press Play again, but slo-mo it."

He did as asked, and as the video ran, I realised what he was talking about. "None of the people in the cars are see through."

"Bingo," said James. "I think we'll want to confirm it and get you there again, maybe in an hour or two."

Will turned to my brother. "Is that really a good idea?"

Angelica nodded. "Yes, it is. We don't know what's going to happen and when. If we can find out a commonality in the who, we'll have more of an idea. If it's going to happen inside the museum, I might be able to get it shut down for a few hours if we can ascertain the time. I have a connection there."

I shook my head. "That's a long shot. How are we supposed to do that?"

Will gave a wry smile. "Do you think you can get it locked down for a week? That should cover the time window."

Angelica smiled. "Unfortunately, not even for me would they do that, and I'm not about to use coercion. The museum shutting down would make the news, and we don't want to panic anyone, not to mention we don't have any proof we can use. Lily's talent is only giving us a rather vague idea at this point. We don't even know if the museum will be the site of the event. Which is why Lily needs to get back there and get more information."

"And she needs to do it quickly," said Sarah. She was taking Imani's role of backing me up while she wasn't here. It was nice to have the support. Luckily, my mother was at the PIB offices today, or I'd have to contend with her worrying unnecessarily too. We had Millicent and Mum keeping a close eye on things because Angelica and James had their hands full with the Chad situation and couldn't be there much. Imani had become James's fill-in and was managing many of the cases. Angelica had Chad's phone and was popping over to him every time it rang so he could answer it. She was close by to zap him if he tried to tell anyone about his situation. We didn't want to push our luck in case he'd found a way around my orders to him to keep it all a secret and pretend everything was normal.

James addressed Angelica. "We need to be at the Natural History Museum by about four because they shut at four thirty. We can establish some kind of radius, see if whatever happens is contained to an area. I also think we should drive in, so we can cover a greater area quickly."

"Agreed." Angelica smoothed a hand over her immaculate bun and met my gaze. "It's unfortunate that your talent doesn't give us a timeline. Because of the risks, I'm going to have to ask you to take our pictures before we go."

I let my head drop, and I rubbed my temples. God, I hated being a witch sometimes. I raised my head and looked at her. "I know." I had to consider myself lucky that she didn't ask this of me every time they went out on dangerous assignments. Maybe they didn't want to know. If there was someone out there who needed to be caught and they had to sacrifice an agent, they weren't going to shy away, but losing the whole team was something else. Whatever this event was going to be, it was going to be huge.

Lavender looked at Angelica. "I think Lily should take video again. We'll compare the workers at the museum from this morning to this afternoon, see if anything changes. Maybe we should follow a couple of them, see where they go afterwards? That might give us a clue."

Angelica nodded slowly. "Very good thinking Agent Belrose. There's high risk associated with doing that, but we can assign two agents to follow each of them, and after we've done that, Lily can take the agents' pictures. If they come back see through, we'll know something is happening soon. If that's the case, I think we'll have to jump in and question the workers about what their movements will be for the afternoon and evening."

Will turned to Angelica. "Are you going to spell them or ask the questions without any interference?"

"I want to keep things as aboveboard as possible, but if it's a choice between breaking the law and saving lives or keeping honest and many people dying unnecessarily, I'll choose option one every day. I know you would too."

"Yes, Ma'am. Always."

"You've brought up an interesting point, though, dear. If it wasn't for Lily's talent foretelling death, we wouldn't need to have this conversation, but I think it brings to light that there are definitely situations where we need to break the law. We all signed up to this job to save lives and bring justice to those who deserve it. That comes before all else. We're doing no harm by manipulating these people into giving us information in this particular case. I don't advocate for it to become an easy way out in every situation. We're treading a thin line that too many witches would cross if they got into the habit. If any of you are using this spell to get information out of people, I want you to make sure that you avoid asking any questions that are unrelated to the specific issue. Tread carefully, lest we become the monsters we wish to incarcerate." She hadn't taken her intense gaze from Will's the whole speech.

He nodded. "Fully understood, Ma'am."

"Good." She looked around at everyone else. "No one uses the truth or coercion spell without my permission. I will also ask you to frame the spells in a very specific way so the magic knows to only let them answer questions pertinent to the investigation. Actually, let's have this conversation now. I never want my honesty or professionalism called into question. We might soon find ourselves in a situation where our integrity is all that saves us." She must be talking about Chad and the directors. If we managed to beat them and survive, there would be other people who'd be asking questions. I didn't know if there was a level of witch law enforcement higher than the PIB. Maybe there was, or maybe it was a group of super-rich people who kept an eye on the witch world in general. I had no idea, but surely there was some kind of group that oversaw everything. "So, we do this carefully, and we have two agents questioning one person. I also want you to promise that you'll undergo interrogation by me under a truth spell in relation to any victim interviews if our integrity is ever called into question. If you can't agree to that, you won't be participating in this investigation." Angelica's magic grazed my scalp. "Do you all agree?"

We all responded in the affirmative, and a little bell chimed. I looked around. Where the hell was that coming from? James laughed. "No one knows where it comes from. It's just one of those things we accept."

"Is it a magic-generated noise, or is a being sitting somewhere holding a bell, and they have to chime it every time? And if so, do they get paid, or is it a labour of love?"

Will grinned. "I doubt someone is sitting there with a bell, Lily, but you never know."

Angelica looked at me, her stern-parent face activated. "Let's get going. I'd like you to start filming as soon as we leave here, dear. We need to establish a radius for a likely attack or accident, if it's possible. And we have a lot of ground to cover." She turned to Will. "You can drive."

"Yes, Ma'am."

Angelica looked at Lavender. "I'd like you to update Agents Jawara and Bianchi. Let them know the specifics of what we're doing. We may need them urgently. Be prepared to contact Agent Roche on short notice, but don't tell him anything unless and until I say."

He gave a nod. "Yes, Ma'am."

Lavender stood and moved to the middle of the room. "Good luck, Lily."

I smiled. "Thanks."

Lavender made his doorway and walked through. Angelica stood and went to the spot Lavender had just vacated. "Everyone stand next to me. Lily, you get into shot too."

We did as asked, and I brought up the photo app on my camera. I got us all into frame as my heart rate escalated. Would we or wouldn't we be ghostly? I swallowed my trepidation. "Say disaster!"

A chorus of "Disaster" rang out, and, funnily enough, we all smiled. I clicked off the shot, even though I hadn't needed to.

Will smiled. "Well, that's a relief. All opaque and accounted for."

James laughed. "I never thought I'd enjoy being called opaque, but there you have it."

"It's all the rage this season." Sarah winked.

Formalities done, I hurried off to the toilet—because who knew when I'd get another opportunity—then joined everyone at the Range Rover. Angelica was in the front, of course. James was in the middle of the back seat next to Sarah who was behind Angelica. I hopped into the remaining seat behind Will and got my phone ready. Once we hit the high street, an ache in my neck from the tension of seeking out soon-to-be-dead people, I started filming.

A couple of minutes later, Will said, "Verdict?"

"Westerham is safe. No ghosties."

"Ghosties?" Will quirked an eyebrow, which I saw via his rear-view mirror.

"Well, ghosts isn't quite right because they're still alive, and we have a chance to change the outcome. Ghosties sounds cute. I have enough horror when I ponder too long on the fact that the real person in front of me is truly temporary. I mean, they're warm, alive, present when I see them, but then, within a week or two, I know they're going to be dead in a box or burnt to ashes, ceasing to exist. I mean, I know we all die, but it's not something we think about every minute of every day. But when I see those people…" I shuddered. "It feels icky, like they're already dead, like I'm looking at a corpse. It's as if a cold, empty energy coalesces around me. It's not quite evil, but it's… scary—a vast, lonely nothingness. I don't like it."

James grabbed my hand and squeezed it before letting go. "I didn't realise it was that bad. Thanks for doing this, Lily."

I shrugged one shoulder. "It's okay. I don't talk about it because what's the point? It must be necessary if the magical realms, or whatever it is, gave it to me. Wanted or not, I have it, so I should use it for the greater good. I suppose if I can use it to help people, it doesn't seem as bad. I can put up with the horror as long as I know something positive sometimes comes from it."

Sarah leaned forward so she could see me past James. "That's a great way of thinking about it." She gave me an encouraging smile. "You're doing so much good, Lily."

I smiled. "Thanks." I looked out the window as fields gave way to another built-up area and steeled myself. "Okay, I'd better get back to it." I held my phone up to the window and started recording again. Thankfully, ten minutes later, nothing out of the ordinary had shown up. I'd seen a couple of older people who were going to die, but that was expected. I did have to fight the urge to tell Will to stop the car so I could jump out and tell them to go do something they'd always wanted but hadn't gotten around to, or tell everyone they loved how they felt—they would have thought I was crazy. They would've been right, but that was beside the point.

The closer we got to London, the more I clenched my jaw. I held my breath and quickly panned the camera around the car, just to make sure no one was about to die. I breathed out my relief in a whoosh.

"I take it we're all going to survive the next week or so?" James asked.

"Yes, probably. Touch wood." Old superstitions died hard, and sometimes people died a day after I saw they were see through, although that could be because I saw them late. I had no idea if my talent had a set ability of being able to tell if someone was going to die in two weeks, or if it was just random. But so far, everyone I'd seen show up see through and had contact with until they died had a death within a few days of me seeing them, so maybe two weeks was generous. Although the exception of everyone dying was Angelica. She'd managed to survive after I'd seen her impending death through my lens. So I knew there was a chance we could make a difference.

I licked my bottom lip. I hoped for our sakes that this event wasn't happening within the next few days. We needed more time to untangle it all.

"Anything out of the ordinary yet, dear?"

"No. I'll let you know as soon as I notice anything." I rolled my shoulders back and stretched my neck, then returned to filming. After another half an hour, I gave them an update. "So far nothing." I yawned. All this time in the car and I was ready for a nap.

"Are we keeping you up?" James nudged me with his elbow.

I gave him an unamused look. "Yes, as a matter of fact. For someone who isn't an agent, I'm sure working a lot."

Angelica didn't turn to look at me. "Even though you're using your talent, which takes less power than many other spells, you've been doing it nonstop for almost an hour. Don't underestimate how much energy you're expending. Just make sure you have a good dinner, and go to bed early."

"You won't get any arguments from me." I yawned again.

Angelica did turn this time, gracing me with a rare smile. "How novel."

James and Will laughed, and Sarah snorted.

I smirked. "Don't worry. I'll save them all up for another day. I'd hate for you to miss out."

"How thoughtful of you, dear."

I grinned. "I know."

Sarah looked at me, then past me, out the window. "Sorry to be such a pain, but…."

"Yeah, yeah. Okay." I hoiked my phone up, stared at the screen, and pressed Record again. "For a new agent, you're a real pain in the butt."

"Just being diligent." I heard the smile in her voice. "I'm trying to be the best agent I can."

"Good attitude, dear. You'll go far." I wasn't sure if Angelica was having a dig at me, but I doubted it. If there was anything in her comment, it would've been in jest. I knew her well enough now to realise how much responsibility she'd given me over time. She would never have done that if she didn't trust me. And she'd been quick to compliment me on some things lately. I should be kinder to myself. I might not be an agent, but I had a lot of experience as a witch, and my abilities hadn't often failed me. I needed to trust the process. Trust myself.

Will drove along a road with modern units on our right and a park on our left. We crossed a concrete suspension bridge over the Thames. I couldn't be sure if I thought the bridge was pretty or not. It had two little golden ships on poles on either side of the beginning of the span, but rust stains, like dirty tears, streaked the white poles. The cable holding the bridge in place was a salmon colour—not my favourite. On the other side, trees continued on one side of us. On the other were buildings and people walking along the footpath. Hmm, a blonde woman dressed in a nurse's uniform was see through. She only looked to be in her early twenties.

A prophetic talon scraped down the length of my spine.

I sat up straighter, my tiredness sloughing off.

I sensed James watching me, and Will, who'd been chatting to Sarah, stopped talking. Either I wasn't the only one who felt the shift, or they were reacting to me. Eventually, we came to a T intersection, a square in front of us. A man in a business suit and green tie stood on the corner in front of a Boss clothing shop, waiting to cross. "That man's see through." A rustle sounded in the car as everyone turned to look, including Will. I panned the phone around to film past James and Sarah, to the footpath beyond.

Will flicked his blinker on. *Click, click. Click, click.* He turned left as I filmed the shops in that direction. A woman in a shop window dressing mannequins was also see through. "There's another one." Everyone looked to that side, but we were already past. "Sorry. Too late."

"Can you slow down a bit, dear? Do a lap of the square."

"Yes, Ma'am." He veered to the right, the lap around the square one-way traffic.

"Where are we in relation to the museum?"

Sarah answered me. "We're just over a mile away. This is Sloane Square in Chelsea."

"Okay. Thanks." It was such a pretty area. Mature trees ringed the square, and character shops with elegant apartments above bordered the street. Black cabs and red double-decker buses drove ahead and behind us. "It's certainly a busy hub. Ah, damn." There was another see-through person. She looked to be in her forties and had on a black skirt and white shirt. A hotel worker or maybe a waitress?

After doing a lap around the square, Will continued straight.

"Stop the car!"

"I can't, Lily. There's nowhere to pullover."

"Don't you have sirens or something? Pretend you're the police."

Angelica's magic tickled my scalp. *Whoop, whoop*—a siren gave a short wail. Red and blue light reflected off the shop windows around us.

"Fine, then," Will grumbled and pulled over.

Angelica waved her hand towards me. My clothes changed. "What the hell?" I had on a police uniform.

"It's going to look weird if a normal person jumps out of a police car and starts taking photos, and I don't trust a no-notice spell. Also, we don't want anyone crashing into the back of us. Hurry, dear. We don't have all afternoon."

I looked behind to make sure I wouldn't be wiped out by a bus when I opened the door. It was all clear. I shoved the door open, jumped out, and ran around the back of the car and back to Barclay's Bank. I stood at the glass doors, getting a good view of the tellers behind their counters. When I'd gotten everything I needed, I made my way back towards the Range Rover, peering into each shop as I went. Then I kept walking, filming into another ten shops past the car. Will slowly followed me, and when I was done, I hopped back in.

Angelica's magic caressed my scalp. My normal clothes replaced the uniform, and the coloured lights disappeared. Will indicated and pulled out into the traffic.

James looked at me. "Are you going to explain?"

"I thought I noticed a teller in the bank was see through, but I couldn't be sure because it was only a glimpse. When I went back, two out of the four tellers were see through, so were the assistants in about one in every four shops." I turned to my window and pressed Record again.

"How many people is that since we started this morning?" A hint of fear came through in Sarah's voice.

"Too many." I hadn't counted, but that was the appropriate answer.

Will turned right. "Give us a ballpark, please."

I took a deep, noisy breath in, then out through my nose. "I don't know. What was this morning's count? Forty-five or forty-seven—I can't remember exactly, but it's a lot. This afternoon, what am I at? Potentially another twelve or fourteen."

James whistled. "That's horrific. What the hell are we looking at?"

"A terrorist or group with guns or knives?" Sarah suggested.

Angelica shook her head. "I don't think so. Maybe just one witch terrorist. Maybe a terrible accident? But if it wasn't a witch, I don't know that Lily's magic would've alerted us."

"But it always shows me when someone is going to die, and they're not always witches. It's often normal people. And it's shown me when someone is going to have a heart attack, so that's not from being attacked."

Will stopped for a red traffic light. "I think we should keep all our options open as to the cause. Also, we have people in two locations, so I'm not convinced that it happens where you've seen them. And do we think all those people have plans to go to the museum on the same day?"

I shrugged. "Maybe there's some kind of event booked for the museum, like a retail-awards thing?"

"But why are so many people in business attire see through?" asked Sarah.

I shook my head. "I don't know." I slumped against the seat, despondency bringing the burn of tears. I blinked them away and focussed on the job at hand—filming out the window.

Angelica put her phone to her ear. "Hello. Yes. Can you check if the Natural History Museum has any private functions booked in the next two weeks? Thanks. Bye." She put her phone on her lap. "Millicent will get back to us."

Will glanced in his rear-view mirror. "We're almost there."

A young guy in a Science Museum uniform stood out the front of the establishment, smoking. But I was pretty sure it wasn't the reason he was going to die. If we didn't stop this impending disaster, he'd never get older and have a chance to get cancer. *Hmm, brain, that wasn't nice.* I shook my head, dislodging the inappropriate thought. Maybe he would've quit and lived till he was one hundred and a great grandfather. Which brought me around to the fact that he would've been early twenties, max. He would likely have parents, possibly siblings, a significant other. They would all be devastated if he died, just like all the other families of all the other people.

Crap.

I blinked away my second bout of tears and kept filming. "Here's the museum."

"I'll go around the block, just so you can get a lay of the land."

"Okay."

The American national anthem started playing. What the hell? Sarah echoed my thoughts. "What in the dickens is that?"

Angelica took another phone out of her pocket. "I have to

run. Sorry. I'll meet you at the museum as soon as I can."
Angelica's magic tickled my scalp; then she was gone.

James put us out of our misery. "Chad's phone."

"Of course he has the US national anthem as his ring-tone." I rolled my eyes.

"I picked him as more of a Britney Spears fan." Sarah giggled.

Will snorted. "I would've said the intro music to *Sesame Street*."

I had to laugh—my awesome peeps knew how to brighten a stressful situation. "Yep, that's more his speed."

James ruined the moment by sharing a serious look with Will in the rear-view mirror. "Let's hope that call was managed safely."

"Was it one of the directors?" I asked.

"Probably," James said. "There are a couple of people from headquarters we're trying not to let go to voicemail too much because they'll get suspicious. His PA is loyal to the directors—she was promoted to that job when Chad came on-board—and she's always checking up on him, or checking with him, rather."

"So she's a helicopter assistant who reports back to the directors?" Why did that surprise me?

"Yes, Lily, that's exactly what she is." James frowned. He and Angelica had a lot on their shoulders with both this case, whatever else the PIB had going on, plus the directors and our speedily approaching clash. What if they'd already put a price on our heads? Maybe they told Chad it might happen if we clue into what they're doing? What if they planned on killing at least a couple of us to ensure we wouldn't be a problem in the future?

My stomach plunged into the sea of panic, and I placed

my free hand on it as I recorded a group of three see-through teens about to cross the road. Will turned right, in front of them, and then we were past, the National History Museum's front façade on our right.

I turned in my seat. "Can you slow down?"

"Okay."

Will slowed, and I stared out the back window. After crossing the road, they didn't go towards the museum; they went down the stairs leading to the South Kensington Underground station. Was something going to happen there? Another man walking who'd come from the opposite direction and went down the stairs just ahead of them wasn't see through. Maybe not. Grrr, this was beyond frustrating. I gritted my teeth and resumed filming out of my window. The black cab behind us beeped, and I jumped. "You can go normal speed now. Sorry."

"That's okay, Lily," Will said as he accelerated. "It's not your fault some people have no manners."

I turned again and looked out the back window at the cab. The driver stuck his middle finger up. My mouth dropped open, and I sucked in a breath. Pressing my lips together, I drew my magic. "Make him feel like he's wet himself." Power surged through my body for a few seconds, and the man's eyes bugged wide. He looked down at his crotch. I smiled and nodded. "That's what you get for being a craphead."

James looked at me. "Did you just cast that spell on the cab driver?"

"Yes. He stuck his finger up at us. Beeping was bad enough and almost understandable, but Will sped up. He needs to check his attitude."

Sarah laughed. "You're hilarious." She twisted around to look at the driver. "He's looking down at his crotch and back to the road, now at his crotch again. How long will the spell last?"

"Oh, I have no idea. I didn't know it was a set and forget." I chuckled.

"He's just veered to the left and almost into the other lane. Oh, he's weaving now."

James's tone held a warning. "*Lily*... as funny as it is, you don't want to cause an accident." He must have seen the look on my face because he said, "Not even a little one."

I sighed. "Fine." I drew more magic and undid the spell. "Happy now?"

He smiled. "Yes, thank you."

Will pulled over. "I'm going to park at the Royal Albert Hall. You guys can get out here and walk. I'll see you up there soon."

James unbuckled his seat belt. "Okay."

Sarah undid hers and opened the door. They both got out, and I shuffled across since they were on the safe side and slid out. I ducked my head back in the car. "See you soon." He gave me a smile and a chin tip. I shut the door, and he drove off. The three of us walked quickly around the corner and past the Science Museum. I filmed the whole way. As we approached the next corner and the stairs to the Underground, a see-through person exited onto the street, and another see-through person started their descent. "I can't shake the feeling that this might have something to do with that tunnel. It would make sense if it isn't the museum itself. So many people walk through it."

"But why would all the people working at Chelsea walk through there?" Sarah asked.

James shrugged. "I'll play devil's advocate and say that they might live around here and catch the Tube." His brow furrowed. "Or it could be the Tube itself, or a station. Terrorists often target public transport… if it's a terrorist. Rail accidents have been known to happen too."

"That's a hell of a lot of ground to cover." Sarah turned right, and we followed her to the front door of the museum.

James paused at the door to let me through first. My brother was such a gentleman. "Which is why doing those interviews is so important." A wave of dizziness swept over me, and I tripped. James grabbed my arm and peered into my eyes, assessing. "Are you all right?"

I took a steadying breath. "Yes. Just tired. I've never filmed using my talent for this long before. Maybe that spell on the cabbie overtaxed me. I think heating his crotch used more energy than I thought it would."

One corner of his mouth quirked up. "That's something I've never heard anyone say, but, somehow, hearing it from you makes total sense."

I grinned. "Meh, I'm one of a kind."

Sarah put her arm around me. "You certainly are, and we love you for it. Are you sure you're okay?"

"Yep. I'll take some video, then, considering we're thinking maybe the Underground could be the place it happens, once I'm done here, I'll sit at the corner opposite the stairs so no one gets sus, and I'll film the entrance. I think recording people who've finished work would be our best bet since they come in at a consistent time every morning. I mean, if I were a terrorist, I'd want to hit at peak hour, and if it's just a random accident, more people are likely to be affected at peak hour, and we have a lot of potential victims. That means we'll be here until at least five thirty."

Confident I wasn't about to keel over, James released my

arm. "Wear a no notice when you do that. We don't want anyone thinking you're impinging on their privacy."

"Fair enough. Okay, I'd best get to it."

I started by filming the workers who were see through this morning. Bummer—still going to die. I sighed and wandered into the cafeteria. One of the women behind the counter was see through. I frowned. The bodies were piling up. Dead crowd walking.

I decided to try something I'd never done—ask my magic how it was going to happen. Would it work? There was only one way to find out. I pointed my phone at the same woman I'd just filmed. "Show me the woman see through if she dies from an accident." My eyes widened. She was solid. Oh my God, this was epic. I had no idea my talent could work that way. I stopped filming. "Show me the woman see through if she dies of an intentional attack." I sucked in a breath. See through. "Does a non-witch cause her death." Solid. Adrenaline pumped through me. This was such a massive discovery, that my magic was capable of this. "Does a witch using magic cause her death." See through.

I hurried back to the entrance, pointed my phone at the workers I'd seen before and asked the same questions. The answers were all clear—this wasn't going to be an accident, and it was going to happen because of a witch. Hmm, could I go even further? "Show me who dies at this museum." They were solid. "Show me who dies on the train." See through. Oh my God. All this time I had this ability and I hadn't known.

We had to stop it. How, I had no idea. Even if we pinpointed which line and which train carriage, we had no idea when... unless my magic could figure that out too. If it couldn't, we could hardly ask whoever ran the Underground to shut it down. If by some miracle someone listened to Angelica and said "okay, we'll shut it down for an hour," that mightn't be enough time. We might get around it if I grabbed one of the people who was see through and we kept asking for different shutdown times until that person wasn't see through anymore, but that would mean giving up my secret. It would also mean that we wouldn't catch whoever was doing this, and they'd surely plan something else. Gah! Why was everything so complicated?

I turned to James, who'd stayed close by my side as I made my way through the museum. Sarah had waited in the main hallway, ready to intercept Angelica when she got back to update her on what we'd decided. "My magic's told me that it's going to happen on the train."

He stared at me, mute for a moment. His eyes lit up. "That's fantastic! I mean, it's not fantastic that it's happening, but you know."

"Yes, I do."

"Did you find out anything else?"

"Not yet, but I can try." I found a see-through person, one of the workers I'd seen earlier. "Show me if they're going to die on the platform." They were see through. "Show me if they're going to die on the train." See through. Hmm. "Show me if they're going to die today." See through. "Show me if they're going to die tomorrow." See through. I listed all the days of the week, one by one, and it was still the same. Then I looked up a few stations before and after South Kensington and asked if it was going to occur at any of those. Still see through. Argh. Seemed as if I'd reached the limit of that particular talent. Crap. I looked at James. "Nope. My magic wouldn't give me a day, and it only narrowed it down to occurring on the train or the platform, but not which train or platform."

James put his hands on his hips. "Could it be both?"

I shrugged. "I suppose. Maybe something blows up while the train's at the station?"

"Maybe, although we don't know which station. Let's keep looking around, just to make sure we've got everything we can. While we're walking, I'll think."

After doing a lap of the ground floor and half the second, dizziness surged over me. I threw an arm out, slapping my palm against the wall I was lucky enough to be standing next to. James grabbed my upper arm. "I think you should sit down. Right now." His magic prickled my scalp. "I've just put a no notice on you. Sit on the floor." For once in my life, I didn't argue. I rested my back against the wall and slid to the floor, his hand stopping me from sliding too quickly.

He sat next to me. "Pass me the phone. Let's see what you have so far." I handed it to him, lowered my head, and shut my eyes. There were so many ghosties on there. If we couldn't stop it, the museum would lose a big chunk of their workforce. That would be devastating to their workmates. The tsunami from this event was going to scour the whole country and even further afield.

Why would someone want to do this?

My stomach growled loud enough that James nudged my shoulder with his. His magic tingled my scalp. "Here, have this."

I opened my eyes and raised my head. He handed me a chocolate cupcake. "Mill made them yesterday. I think that'll make you feel better."

I smiled, put my nose near the handful of chocolate yumminess, and sniffed. "Mmm, I think it will. Thank you, big brother."

He smiled. "My pleasure. Can't have you fainting on us. What would Mum say?"

I chuckled. "Yeah, you'd be in her bad books for at least a week."

"And no one needs that." He gave me a wry smile.

I bit into the cupcake. "Oh, man, it's so good."

"It's rude to talk with your mouth open." Angelica stood there, one eyebrow raised as she looked down at me. Will and Sarah were with her, both smirking. There was a strong family resemblance.

I took another bite out of my cupcake and purposely spoke around it, opening my mouth so they would be suitably disgusted. "You guys have the same smirk, and you're really good at sneaking up on people." Not that I was super alert. The cupcake had all my attention, and rightly so.

Will ignored my comparison. "Why are you eating a cupcake?"

James answered, denying me another opportunity to talk with a full mouth. "She's exhausted, and then her stomach started complaining. If I didn't feed her, she would've collapsed." He made a bubble of silence. "I'm going to lend her some power later too."

I swallowed the last of the treat. "You don't have to do that. What if you need it tonight?"

He shook his head. "I'll be fine, and we need that information ASAP. It's either that or you'll magic yourself into the ground and end up spending a week in bed."

Angelica's poker face softened just enough that I could tell she'd only just realised what they'd asked of me. "I forget you're not indestructible sometimes, dear. I should've thought of that."

I waved my hand. "Don't worry. I don't speak up because I

want to get the job done. I'm probably old enough that I should learn how to manage myself better. Next time, I'll ask. I didn't envisage using my talent so much would make me this tired. I've acclimatised to using a lot of magic, and this isn't supposed to use much."

Angelica cocked her head to one side. "It depends how you use your talent. Taking photographs is a moment of magic, but videoing is constant, and you're drawing from the river of power as well. Holding any type of spell for an extended period is taxing, no matter what it is."

James stood. "And she's discovered a new skill with that talent." He explained about the locations and that it would be an intentional attack.

Angelica, Will, and Sarah gazed at me, astonishment radiating from their faces. "Well, dear, there you go, impressing me once again. Delving that deeply into the future takes a lot of energy, and on top of what you've already done, well, no wonder you're exhausted."

My cheeks warmed from the praise. "Thanks."

James looked around, then at Angelica. His feet moved, as if he wanted to hurry and get things done. "We're going to camp out near the railway entry between five and five thirty. Lily can video everyone who commutes at peak hour, and I think we should follow two or three of them. It'll narrow down where they go afterwards, which line they use."

"Okay. I'm glad we know where to target our efforts." Angelica gave me another smile.

James nodded; then his phone rang. He answered it. "Hey, Mill. Yes...." He listened for a minute. "Okay, thanks. Bye." He looked at Angelica. "She's just confirmed there's filming booked in this coming weekend, which wouldn't have any of those people we saw, and the staff won't be here. The film people bring their own catering and staff. Next week, on Tuesday night, they have a Charity dinner, but it's for the European elite. I doubt any of the retail workers we saw today will attend. It just confirms what we're thinking."

Will ran a palm down his cheek. "Agreed. And it won't take long to discover which train they catch. Hopefully, the people we follow are consistent in where they sit on the way home. We need to narrow this down." No one argued with Will's accurate and depressing assessment.

James handed my phone to Angelica, and she watched the footage I'd just taken. It was nice to just sit and recharge without having to ask. She probably could've waited until later, but she chose now, and I was pretty sure why. Just when I thought she couldn't surprise me….

Angelica and Will had a quiet conversation, which I didn't really pay attention to. I was busy staring at nothing, trying to regain some energy, so when Will said, "I'm going to get the car. See you soon," I had to play catch up.

I looked up at Angelica. "Why's Will getting the car? I thought we were staying."

"I want you sitting in the car observing. It's more comfortable."

"Thank you."

"It's not just for you, dear. If you're in the Range Rover, it will be easier for you to share James's power without any witches noticing. Doing that out in the street is just asking for trouble."

I grinned. Some things in life were consistent—Angelica's bluntness was oddly comforting. "Fair enough. Everyone wins."

"Indeed."

James helped me stand, and Angelica handed my phone

back. We made our way downstairs and to the street. The Tube-station entrance was on a corner. We crossed the road there and hopped into the waiting black SUV. Will had parked on the footpath. "I've put a no-notice on it. Any witches who see it will just assume we're law enforcement."

"Sounds good to me." I settled into my comfy leather seat in the back, where I'd sat before.

"We'll wait till four thirty. Let you regain some energy, dear. It will also give us a chance to catch more of the people we need to, confirm what your magic has told us."

So we waited.

When it was time to film again, James grabbed my hand. "I'm good to go."

"Thanks." I gave him a grateful smile. "Tell me when you've had enough."

"Will do. My portal's open when you're ready."

It had been a while since I'd channelled through someone else, so I closed my eyes to better concentrate. I called to James's power through our skin-to-skin connection. The warmth of his magic seeped through my palm, a trickle at first. It soon flowed freely, and I pointed my phone to the stairs leading to South Kensington Tube Station. I took a deep breath and pressed Record.

Sarah leaned forward, giving her a clear view across the car and out my window. "Are those museum workers see through?"

"Two of them are, and they were before. The third isn't. I don't remember seeing him before, so he probably wasn't."

"Agents Blakesley, get out and follow them," Angelica said.

"Yes, Ma'am," they both said. They didn't muck around either. They jumped out of the Range Rover, ran across the road, and disappeared down the stairs. Some of my nerves dissipated when it was clear they were solid.

"They're not see through." I figured it was good to give Angelica an update.

"Thank you, dear. I would imagine you'd be running after them if they were."

I smiled. "Yep."

After five minutes, she turned around to look at me. "You can stop filming. We'll wait till they get back. Let's see what they say."

I stopped filming and released James's hand. "Thanks, bro. That was a huge help."

He smiled. "Any time."

I put my phone on my lap and looked at Angelica. "How did the Chad thing go before? Who was calling?"

Her lip twitched up into an almost sneer, revealing her disdain. "His assistant. He took the call and behaved. So far, so good." I would've asked her if she was worried about tomorrow, but she would say no, whether she was or not.

Before long, Will and Sarah returned. Angelica got me to film more people, and Will and Sarah had to follow them. Once they'd done that, they got back in the car, and Will started it and pulled out into the traffic.

Angelica made a bubble of silence. "So, verdict?"

Sarah clicked her belt in. "Everyone we followed caught the Circle Line. They were going towards Gloucester Road rather than Sloane Square. So they likely come from that direction in the morning."

"So now what?" I asked.

Angelica kept her gaze forward, her voice devoid of emotion. "I don't know, Lily. We need more time."

I sucked in a breath. We might not have more time, and if

Angelica wasn't sure what our next move should be, what hope did we have?

There was only one conclusion I could make—things weren't going well.

Not well at all.

CHAPTER 4

The late afternoon sun kissed the back of my neck as I rested my head on my arms. The picnic table in Angelica's back garden was the perfect place to recharge my flagging energy levels. Eyes closed, I concentrated on my breaths—in, out, in, out. Sleep had almost claimed me when there was a soft tap, tap, tap on my ear. I sat up slowly and wiped off the dribble that had collected at the side of my mouth.

I smiled. "Hello, Pipsqueak. How are you?"

The squirrel I'd named recently chittered, and an image of almonds came into my head.

"Always hungry. Okay." I magicked some almonds from the pantry onto the table, then regretted it as dizziness whooshed through me. "Crap. I have to be careful. Why don't I think first?" Pipsqueak peered at me for a moment. But his priority wasn't working out what the hell I was talking about. He turned and grabbed an almond, ripped the brown skin off it, and tucked into the creamy flesh. As adorable as he was, nibbling away, exhaustion demanded I put my head back on my arms on the tabletop and shut my eyes.

After a few minutes, a small someone who weighed not much climbed along my arm and up to my shoulder. I smiled. Cute companions were comforting. Try saying that quickly five times. I did.

"What are you mumbling about?"

I sat up slowly as Will plonked next to me on the bench seat. "Tongue twister."

He stared at me but said nothing. Eventually he chuckled. "I'm not even going to ask you to elaborate. I'm probably better off not knowing."

I shrugged. "Up to you." I blinked and whipped my head around to the squirrel on my left shoulder. He looked at me. I looked at him. His big round eyes didn't shy away from my widened ones. "What did you do?"

A happy feeling of ownership came from him, but I couldn't fully marvel over it because I was too busy quietly freaking out. Ew, wee alert. Gross.

"What's wrong?" Will's brow furrowed.

"Karma. This little pain in the butt just weed on me." I magicked it away—the wee, not the squirrel. "Please don't do that again. I'm not your territory. I don't need marking."

Will laughed.

"*Yes. Yes, yes, yes, yes, yes, yes. Mine, mine, mine, mine.*" Pipsqueak didn't have the vocabulary of some of the other squirrels or Abby, but I understood him just fine.

"No, no, no, no, no, no, no. Seriously, just no. In my world, we don't pee on our friends."

Will snorted. I glared at him.

The squirrel cocked his head to one side, possibly trying to figure out what the meaning of all this was. Dampness seeped through my T-shirt again. Damn it! Looked like he wasn't getting the point.

Or maybe he was, and he was a recalcitrant squirrel.

I magicked the wee away and sighed, then yawned. For goodness' sake, there were so many tiny ways I used my magic every day that it was now second nature, but I was going to put myself into a coma if I wasn't careful. "I think I need a nap for a few days."

He put his arm around me, pulled me into his side, and kissed my temple. "I'd say get to it, but we'll probably need you later. Maybe keep the nap to an hour. And you can use my power next time. Angelica's worried that whatever is going to happen might happen tomorrow morning. We might only have tonight to work it out. Of course, we can't be sure, but we need to be ready for every peak-hour service until whatever we're waiting for eventuates."

"I figured that. If we only have tonight, well, it's not enough time." My shoulders sagged, and the squirrel leaped onto the table. *Yep, save yourself from this sinking ship, Pipsqueak.*

"Howdy, folks."

Will and I both turned. "Lavvie, baby." I pushed off the table and stood. He gave me a hug.

"How's my favourite witch?"

"I thought I was your favourite." Sarah walked out behind him and pouted.

"You were my favourite, but Lily has that adorable Aussie accent."

Sarah rolled her eyes. "Fine. I can't compete with that. As long as I'm your second favourite."

He blew her a kiss. "You know it."

Will stood. "What's up?"

Lavender raised a well-manicured brow. "Ever the perceptive one. Not much gets past you."

"It doesn't. So, spill." Normally, I would've said Will was kidding, but his expression was in poker mode.

Sarah put a calming hand on Will's arm. "It's Ma'am's idea, not his, so go easy."

Full credit to Lavender, he didn't back down. He stood in front of Will, his body language relaxed, arms loose at his sides, hands dangling. "I need Lily to accompany me on a little trip." He made a bubble of silence. "I think I've worked out how to mask the spell signature that might give us away to the directors. I want to give it a trial run, and since Lily's the only one who can order Chadiot around, I need her. Ma'am's busy at the moment—she's planning to interview two disgruntled rail employees that your mother uncovered. There've been two firings in the past two months, and both men threatened that there would be payback. Ma'am's looking into them."

"As long as Lily isn't in danger and doesn't have to cast any spells, you can have her. But I'm coming with you."

"Wow, thanks for your permission." I scowled at Will. "I know you care about me, but I'm not a possession."

His expression didn't change. "I know, but when it comes to your safety, I won't apologise for being careful or bossy. This comes under PIB business, so I think it's only logical I intervene where I feel it appropriate. Your personal life is another matter, Lily. When do I ever boss you around when it's not related to work?"

Damn man had a point. "Never. Okay, fine. But try and avoid talking about me like I'm an object or not even here. There is such a thing as professional courtesy."

"I hate to interrupt your lovers' tiff, but time's a wasting."

Lavender pointed to his wrist and a non-existent watch on his freakishly hairless arm.

"Do you wax your arms?" I couldn't help but ask. I knew him well enough to know he wouldn't get offended.

"Of course, darling. My legs and p——"

Will's eyes widened in what I would describe as horror, and he held up a "stop" hand. Ah, my conservative English boyfriend. So cute when he was rattled.

Lavender smirked. "…other places too. I was going to say privates." He rolled his eyes. "Sheesh, peach. Settle, petal."

"As amusing as torturing Will is, can we do this now so I can get back ASAP and have a bit of a sleep?"

Lavender nodded. "James has the coordinates. He and Angelica are insisting one of them makes our doorway because they don't want to give away any secrets." Angelica had explained it to me before, and it made sense, so I didn't ask for an explanation. We followed Lavender inside.

"I have something I need to take care of, but I'll see you guys back here later." Sarah made her doorway in the kitchen and left, and we continued into the living room. James greeted us all and made the doorway. We went straight through to Angelica's country house. I was the only one of us who'd been here before, so I showed them through to the lounge room and the caged idiot.

Hmm, I narrowed my eyes as his gaze met mine. There was something I couldn't quite place. "I'm watching you, Chadiot."

"Enjoy it while you can. I'll get out of here soon, and you'll all pay dearly. Wait till the directors find out what you did."

"Hmm, we'll be waiting a while since you can't say anything, but if it makes you feel better to dream, go right ahead." Hmm, could I order his subconscious to make him dream of swarms of spiders? Or what about making him dream he was being stung by lots of bees that had my face. Ooh, an even better one would be him having to follow Angelica around and do what she said 24/7 because I knew how much he'd love that.

"Lily." Will nudged me with his elbow.

"Oh, sorry. I was off with the torture fairies."

"What? That's a new one. Should I be worried?"

"No, not you." I slowly panned my gaze from Will to Chad, then left it there and waggled my eyebrows.

Lavender walked up to the cage, then looked back at me. "So, honey, I need him out here so I can examine him. Can you make it safe?"

"He's got a magic-blocking bracelet on, and Will's here to stop any physical violence—not that Chad poses much of a threat from that quarter."

Lavender smiled and nodded. "Agreed."

Chad stood and folded his arms before slamming them onto his chest. "I'm a trained agent, I'll have you know."

I rolled my eyes, more for effect than anything. I just loved riling him up. "Yes, yes, we know." I stared at him and stood next to his cage. "You're trained in lots of things, but you're no good at any of them. Isn't that right?"

"No, no it's not!"

It was time to lay down the law. "You're not to hurt Lavender. You're not to touch Lavender. You're to do whatever he asks. Understood?"

He scowled at me.

"Answer me."

His mouth twisted, and his eyes exuded fury and frustration. "Yes. Understood."

I was about to unlock the cage when I realised that I didn't have the key. I turned to Lavender. "Have you got the key?"

"Yes." He took it out of his pocket and stuck it in the lock. Because the cage blocked magic, he couldn't see Chad's aura in there, so we had to do everything the riskier way and bring Chad out. Not that Chad was any kind of threat wearing that bracelet, but just when you thought nothing could go wrong, it did. The fewer chances we took, the better.

"Come out of there and stand here." I pointed next to Lavender and moved out of reach. Will, on the other hand, loomed closer and stood ready, hands by his sides. Will's aura glowed, indicating his portal to the magic river was open and waiting.

Chad moved stiffly, his mouth firmly closed, jaw bunched —his reluctance to do as he was told obvious. Now he knew how we'd felt the whole time he was in charge. Can't say I had any sympathy for him.

Lavender's magic tingled my scalp as he looked over Chad and likely studied the squiggles that represented the spell. Would he be able to hide it properly? If not, how long could we hold off on sending Chad to the directors before they came looking for him? I feared Angelica was right when she said we'd only have a day. Why did everything have to be so time sensitive?

I had no idea how long Lavender would take, and Will was watching Chad like a cat observing a mouse, so I wandered to the country-style kitchen with its marble benchtops and gorgeous white farmhouse sink and stared out the window. How did Angelica keep those formal gardens so neat if she wasn't here? Did she have a gardener, or had she spelled the plants to grow a certain way or stop growing? My legs wobbled with fatigue, a warning not to be ignored.

There was a round breakfast table in front of french doors on the other side of the kitchen. I shuffled over and sat on one of the chairs. Sweet, sweet relief. I lay my head on my arms on the table, Lavender's magic tingling my nape. Hopefully he was working everything out, and quickly. The urge to go home to bed overwhelmed me—the only thing stopping me from leaving was the fact that I didn't have the energy to make a doorway. I probably could if I had to, but considering I needed something in reserve for later, I wasn't willing to try. Instead of worrying about it, I shut my eyes, and my breathing slowed.

"Lily. Lily? Hello. Are you awake?" Will's voice, slight pressure on my back. Maybe his hand?

"Huh?" I sat up slowly. Will and Lavender were staring at me. "How long have I been asleep?"

Will shrugged. "You've been in here for thirty minutes."

"Oh, wow. I've probably managed a twenty-five-minute nap. Yay me. I needed that."

Lavender cocked his head to the side. "Sweetie, going by the bags under your eyes, you still need way more, and maybe some concealer."

"Well, if nobody needed my services, I'd sleep for two days, no problems. How'd you go with Chadiot?"

Lavender smiled. "Success!"

Even Will's poker face had relaxed into a pleased expression. "He's managed to hide it so well that even I couldn't tell."

I held up my hand for a high five. Lavender obliged. "So how did you do it?"

He made a bubble of silence. "I studied the spell and found another one that looks almost identical. Then I cast the other spell, making sure it lined up with the first one. There's one small line in the middle that's different, and the directors will see that and think it's harmless."

"What's the spell?"

There was an unmistakable twitch to his lips. "It's a spell to flatten moobs."

I snorted. "Oh my God. You're joking?"

Lavender shook his head, the laughter finally escaping. "No! It's perfect."

"So, the directors are going to think he's self-conscious about his man boobs, which he doesn't really have." I snorted. This was a total win. We'd gone from thinking it was a rare chance to cover that spell to Lavender having worked something out pretty quickly. "You're pretty damn impressive."

"Yep. I think I've outdone myself. It was tricky to cover one with the other and make it all look like one spell, but the similarity in the signatures is unbelievable. The universe made it so easy for me. The directors are going to respect him even less."

"If that's possible." Will smirked. "You really have a talent for it though. I don't know any other witch who could've placed a signature in an aura so precisely."

A yawn snuck up on me and was out of my mouth before I could cover it with my hand. "Oops, sorry."

Will's mirth turned to concern. "You need more sleep. Let's get you home."

"Is Chadiot locked up?"

"Yes." Will pulled my chair out, which was quite a feat since I was still sitting in it. "Angelica called earlier, and she's going to come and feed him in an hour. Before that, we're having a meeting at her place."

"How am I supposed to sleep and be in the meeting?"

"You're not. You sleep, we meet. I'll update you afterwards."

I eyed him sceptically. "Do you promise to tell me everything?"

"Yes."

"Hmm, I don't believe you, but I'm too tired to argue. Please take me home."

"Your wish is my command." True to his word, he made a doorway, took me home, and even carried me up to bed. Despite the tempest of turmoil raging around us, I felt like the luckiest girl in the world. I could protect myself a lot of the time, but knowing he was looking out for me brought me peace.

Nothing could touch me while I slept in our bed. I held that thought as I drifted off to sleep because soon enough, I would have to leave my haven, and then all bets were off.

Dreamer Lily wished she could stay here forever, safe and oblivious. Logical Lily knew that was impossible.

Damn you, Logical Lily. Why do you always have to be right?

CHAPTER 5

"Lily, wake up."

Will had become my own personal alarm clock. I stretched my arms up and opened my eyes. "What time is it?"

"Seven in the morning."

I sat up, shedding my fatigue. "What?! You weren't supposed to let me sleep that long. Didn't Angelica need me last night? And you promised to tell me everything."

His voice was soothing but firm. "Hey, hey, it's all right. You haven't missed anything. We had to get our ducks in a row. You'll get your chance to help out this morning. Do you feel up to it?"

"Yes. I'm normal tired. A good night's sleep was all I needed." My stomach growled as loudly as we were talking.

"Hmm, I don't think that's quite right… at least not if your stomach has anything to say about it. Get dressed, and we'll grab a quick breakfast. After that, we have a theory to test out."

"Oh? Do tell."

"I'll explain over breakfast." He gave me a quick kiss and slid out of bed. Will's magic tingled my scalp, and his uniform appeared on his body. "Coffee and food will be waiting for you." He opened the door and stepped out. "Don't dawdle."

"Yes, boss."

His chuckle filtered through as he shut the door. He loved it when I called him that. So easy to please, that man.

I dressed in my uniform as well, assuming since Will put his on that this wasn't going to be an incognito outing. The morning was already warm, and for once, I was regretting having to wear a jacket. Maybe I was finally acclimatising? I picked up my phone and checked the weather. Oh, it was already twenty-four degrees Celsius, with a top temperature of thirty-one expected today. That was practically apocalyptic weather for the UK. So I wasn't acclimatising—it was actually going to be hot. Oh well.

By the time I got to the kitchen, Angelica, Imani, Mum, and James were already there, chatting and eating. "Morning, darling." Mum stood and gave me a hug. "Will's made your coffee, and you have a choice of toast, eggs, tomatoes, and bacon, or pancakes, or a bit of everything."

"Hmm, it's a pancakes kind of morning, I think."

I sat next to Imani because Will was next to James, and Angelica and my mother each had a head of the table. Imani turned towards me. "How are you, love? I heard you had a rough day yesterday."

I inhaled the scent of coffee before having a sip. "Mmm, that's good." Priorities. "Um, it wasn't rough per se. It was just a long day with a slow drain of power. Nothing bad happened, and my twelve-hour sleep fixed everything."

"Well, I'm glad you're feeling better."

Mum slipped a couple of pancakes onto my plate. "Thanks, Mum."

"You're welcome." Hmm, Mum was in a good mood, and she was being particularly nice to me—not that she was always awful, but we'd had a rough time adjusting to each other. She wasn't who she used to be, and I guessed I wasn't either. She also seemed calmer this morning. I didn't have the brainpower to contemplate why, so I looked at Angelica. "What's on for today? Will was supposed to update me, but he hasn't had a chance."

"Well, dear, late last night, we brought in the two disgruntled employees for questioning—they both happen to be witches. One wrote a threatening letter to his boss after he was fired, and the other made verbal threats to several of his workmates the day he was dismissed."

"Did they wonder why they were being hauled in so far after the fact?"

"They were both dismissed within the last six weeks and have been interviewed and given a warning by the police, so they were surprised to be called in now, but we don't have to explain ourselves. So we didn't." She gave me a self-satisfied smile.

"Ah, fair enough. And what's the plan for today?" I poured maple syrup on my pancakes. Saliva exploded inside my mouth, which I hadn't closed, and spurted across the table onto James's bacon.

He looked up at me, disgust and sorrow on his face. "My bacon. You've ruined my bacon," he fake-cried.

I laughed. "Sorry. It wasn't intentional. Here...." I drew my magic. "Remove all my saliva from James's bacon." I smiled. "There you go. It's been decontaminated."

He smiled. "Thank you."

Angelica cleared her throat and gave us both a look. "As I was trying to say, your mother called one of my contacts at the museum, and she's managed to get us a list of all the employees with their photos. James has matched the ones that were see through with the list, and we have addresses, which means we can narrow down where the crime is going to occur. The fact that three of our victims catch the Tube from Notting Hill Gate means we're looking at the incident occurring between there and Sloane Square. None of the victims on the museum list appear to live closer than Notting Hill Gate. I could be wrong, but we haven't had time to gather addresses from any of the retailer-worker victims. We're keeping the sacked rail workers locked up today, and you're going to take photos of a couple of our likely victims as they leave for work this morning. If one of our suspects is the guilty party and it was going to happen today, they will no longer be see through."

"But if they're still ghosties?" There was a good chance that neither of them were our suspects, or that they weren't planning on striking today. "And why hasn't James interviewed them? He can just ask them if they're planning anything." My brother's lie-detecting talent was made for this situation.

Angelica pressed her lips together, and the fact that she and James shared a meaningful look didn't escape my notice. "They both refused to talk to him and asked for a solicitor. Their solicitors won't arrive until working hours. If we can find out this morning that we have it in hand and the disaster is no longer happening, I'll feel much better."

Bummer that they refused to talk. "Okay. But if neither of them are our guys, we're back to square one."

"You could say that, yes." She sipped her tea, but her calmness wasn't fooling me. I would've bet a year's worth of double-chocolate muffins that this was messing with her. She'd devoted her life to helping people, seeking justice. To know such a tragedy was racing towards us with no way to stop it would've been beyond frustrating and depressing.

Someone knocked on the reception-room door. "That must be Lavender." Imani stood. "I'll get it."

I looked at James. "Why is he here? Is he coming with us?"

"No, dear. He's helping me with Chad. The spell Lavender put on him yesterday was a test and only temporary because it takes energy to hold it in place. I'll need you to come with us, just so you can give Chad some last-minute instructions. We don't want to leave anything to chance."

"I'd better get eating, then." Sounded like this morning was going to be super busy. Maybe I should have a third pancake. As I stabbed my fork into one and dragged it over to my plate, Imani returned with Lavender. "Morning."

"Good morning, all." He rubbed his stomach. "If only I hadn't already had my porridge. This looks like a lovely spread."

Mum smiled. "Feel free to join us. There's plenty to go around."

He ran a hand over his small, perky bottom. "That's okay, thanks. You don't think this figure keeps itself. There's suffering involved."

I laughed. "I don't think you suffer too much. You shovelled it in like the rest of us in Venice."

"And I'm still paying for it." I gave him a "you have to be kidding me" look, and he blew me a kiss. "When do you want to get this show on the road, Ma'am?"

"We can depart when Lily finishes her breakfast."

I wasn't sacrificing a full tummy to leave earlier, so I just chewed faster and fewer times before I swallowed. My stomach would have to do most of the digestion work, but I was sure it was more than capable.

After scoffing the third pancake, I stood. "Ready to roll."

My mother looked at me, her expression earnest, leaning towards anxious. "Be careful."

I gave her a reassuring smile. "I will. This won't be dangerous. Chad's got no access to magic, and I could probably beat him up if I tried." He wasn't the fittest of people or the smartest; he was also slow to realise things. Not that I wanted to beat him up—I'd probably break my fist if I actually tried, although I could kick him in the b—

"What are you doing, Lily?" Angelica stood staring at me, her mouth arranged in a frown.

"Oops. Sorry." I stepped around my chair and followed them into the hallway. Angelica made a doorway, and I stepped through, then Lavender, then Angelica. Not wanting to get into more trouble for time wasting, I hurried into the living room. Chad was in his cage, scowling—just as I remembered him from the last two times I'd visited. "You're always such a joy to behold."

"The feeling's mutual." He bared his teeth in a parody of a smile. I couldn't blame him for being angry, but he'd earned his place here. "When I get out of here, you're all going down." He stared at me, then behind me where Angelica and Lavender were likely standing.

I held my hand up and made a duck mouth with my hand and touched my fingers and thumb together as if it were talking. "Blah, blah, blah, blah. If it makes you feel better, you keep telling yourself that. Today, however, you're going to go to that meeting with the directors and pretend everything is as they wish. You will not say anything about being kidnapped, imprisoned, or being cut off from your magic. You will not say anything negative about Angelica or any of our group. You will tell them that everything is going as planned. You will act as you normally do." I turned to Angelica. "Does that cover everything?"

She nodded. "I think so, dear. Thank you." She looked at Lavender. "You can do your thing now. Are you sure you can hold it until lunchtime?"

"Yes, Ma'am. Positive."

She gave a nod and unlocked the cage.

"Out you come," I said.

He slowly made his way out. Lavender stood close to Chad and drew his magic. After whispering a few words, Lavender leaned even closer and peered at the symbol. "Hmm."

"What is it?" Angelica asked.

"I'm not sure. Hang on."

Chad glanced at me, then to his cage, as if he wanted to get back to it rather than away. Huh? I narrowed my eyes at him. "What's going on, Chad? What are you worried about?"

He blinked but didn't answer. Sweat broke out on his forehead. "I— I'm worried the directors will notice something's not right and fire me." Why wasn't he skiting that we were all going to die? Surely this wouldn't be the first thing he'd worry about. Chad was all about Chad, but something didn't sit right. Angelica and Lavender looked at each other, revealing they felt the same way I did.

"Chad, pull your pants down and moon us."

Angelica and Lavender looked at me as if I were mad, but they held their tongues.

Chad slowly undid his belt, his cheeks reddening. His hands paused; then his fingers haltingly undid his button, then reached for his zipper. He stared at us, one by one. I raised a brow as if to say "hurry up." Chad slid the zipper down in halting increments. His fingers gripped his waistband and prepared to shove his clothing down. Maybe I'd misjudged the situation. We'd all regret it if I had.

Chad's cheeks puffed up as he drew in a huge breath, then held it. Sweat beaded on his forehead. Just as his cheeks reached maximum redness, the breath exploded out of him with a pop. His chin dropped to his chest, and he sobbed. "I can't do it. I can't moon you." Angelica and I looked at each other, her raised eyebrow mirroring mine. Thank God I'd been right because there were some things you could never unsee. Chad looked up at us, tears spilling over the rim of his eyes. "The spell was on a time limit. It ran out about an hour ago."

Ah, crap. That was the sound of our day going straight to hell.

Angelica's jaw muscles flexed. "Well, there's no way we can send you to that meeting now." She flung an arm out and pointed to the cage. "Get back in there right now before I force you in the most unpleasant way I can think of."

His eyes widened, and he slunk back into his enclosure.

Angelica turned to Lavender and me. "You two can return home. Please let James know what's happened. Tell him to come here, please."

"Yes, Ma'am," I said.

Lavender and I walked to the middle of the lounge room, made our doorways, and left. How the hell was Angelica going to deal with this? How long could she pretend Chad was missing before the directors suspected we were involved?

I doubted it was going to be long at all.

After updating James and sending him on his way, I looked at Will and Imani through my phone and made sure they weren't see through. When that was done, Will's magic tingled my scalp, and he cast a no-notice spell on himself. "You need to do the same. We're travelling to an unusual location. It will only just be opening when we walk out, so we're going to look odd exiting at that time."

"Where are we going?"

"A gym."

Imani smiled. "It's the closest toilet to where we need to go, and it's clean. We're travelling in style today, love. First class all the way."

I laughed. "Yay, us!" What had my life become when I rejoiced at toilet quality?

Within five minutes, we'd stepped through into cubicles and then out through the front door, onto a busy London street. Will guided us three blocks. "They live in that building just there." He pointed to a three-storey older-style block. "Our guy and his girlfriend both catch the Tube together. She works as a secretary at a law firm that's two stops past his."

I wiped sweat off my brow. Today was going to be a scorcher. "So, he gets off at South Kensington, and she gets off one after Sloane Square?"

"Yes," Will confirmed.

We didn't have long to wait before the couple appeared outside their digs and strolled past us. It was easy to follow them because they were both non-witches. Looking at them through my phone camera confirmed that they were both going to die. "Bummer."

Imani's forehead wrinkled. "Bad news, love?"

"I'm afraid so. They're both in trouble."

Will pulled his phone out and made a call. "Hello,

Ma'am. Yes. Lily's just confirmed they're both see through." He listened as we followed the couple across a road and along the next block. "Okay. Will do. Bye." He turned to Imani and me. "She wants us to follow them, find out what carriage they get on, and she wants Lily to take photos of everyone in that carriage. Maybe we can narrow this right down."

"Consider it done."

"Take a photo of yourself first, love. You've photographed Will and me, but not yourself."

"Okay." As we walked, I held my phone up and pressed the little icon that turned the camera around. "I'm all good. Nothing ghostie about me. I'm as solid as a chocolate chip."

Imani chuckled. "That's a random comparison."

"Lily's as random as they come." Will grinned.

"Just so you know, I'm taking that as a compliment, even if it's not meant as one. You can't keep a squirrel-loving Aussie down."

Imani snorted. "We wouldn't have it any other way, love." I was hearing that a lot lately. Was that a good or a bad thing?

Will magicked us travel cards and handed one to me. I was about to ask why we hadn't paid, but he knew me too well. "Don't worry. The PIB is paying for this. We keep these on hand in one of the filing cabinets at work."

We went down the stairs, through the gates, and followed the couple to their platform. Warm wind pushed into our faces. Any moment the train would appear out of the dark tunnel. My heart beat faster. I held my phone up and looked at Will and Imani through it. Still solid. Alive. Safe.

Then the train appeared, slowing until it filled the tracks adjoining the platform. I pointed my camera towards the couple and almost threw up. The crowd of people in business suits who'd gathered at the doors, waiting for them to open, were all faded versions of themselves.

This was a horror I almost couldn't fathom.

I started videoing and panned the phone around to the other carriages. Many people from the adjoining carriages front and rear were going to die. The further to the rear I filmed, the less were see through, until the last two carriages, which were spared the disaster.

Will and Imani moved towards the doors to get on, but I froze. That was a train of death, and I just couldn't bring myself to get on, even though I knew this wasn't the fateful trip. As they reached the doors, Will must've realised I wasn't with them. He turned and opened his mouth to probably tell me to get a move on, but he stopped, then grabbed Imani's arm, preventing her from boarding. When she saw my face, her eyes widened. They both hurried over as the train pulled away.

"Jesus, love. You look like you've seen a ghost. Are you all right?"

I shook my head. "No, for once in my life, I'm not all right."

Deep grooves appeared in Will's forehead—he knew I wasn't one for drama and that I usually sucked it up and kept going, so this must've worried him. "Show me." I handed him the phone, and he pressed Play.

"Oh my God." Imani's hand curled into a fist, and she drew it to her mouth.

Will's voice betrayed his shock. "I've never seen anything like this. Holy Jesus, Mother Mary, and Joseph."

"You're missing a few. Do you want to invoke Buda, Ganesha, or maybe Apollo?" I was handling the horror the only way I knew how—with humour.

Will stared at me but thankfully said nothing. He knew me well enough to get it, but it was telling that he wasn't willing to join in on the joking. "Let's get back to Angelica's. I'm calling a meeting."

"What if this is *the* train, as in now, this trip?"

Will's Adam's apple bobbed as he swallowed. "We'll have to cross our fingers that it's not. There's nothing we can do about it now." My skin prickled with heat. My queasy stomach heaved, and I only just kept everything down.

Imani and I jogged after Will. But no matter how fast we ran, I doubted we could stop this catastrophe in time. And this was one race we could ill afford to lose. If we didn't catch whoever was responsible, it could be the worst tragedy suffered by the Brits since the Second World War. What would that do to Angelica, to Will, to James, and Imani? Would failing these people spell the end of the PIB? It would give the directors an excuse to say the PIB wasn't fit for purpose, not to mention the guilt on everyone's shoulders from all those deaths—deaths that could've been prevented if only we'd figured it out.

Please don't be today.

This could be the moment that destroyed everyone I loved. Would the magnitude of this be enough to make Angelica risk her life and those of my friends in the hopes of preventing it? That was, if we got that chance?

I hadn't thought I could feel any sicker than when I saw the crowd at the train doors, but I was wrong.

Very. Very. Wrong.

CHAPTER 6

Despite the risk of being spied on at the PIB—the directors might have bugged the place—Angelica had taken Will's desire for a meeting and run with it after she confirmed there'd been no mass tragedy on the Circle Line. My relief was short-lived, however, because the disaster could happen this afternoon.

Angelica called us all into the conference room. My mother and Millicent joined us, and even Beren and Liv had cut their mental-recouperation time off to come in. They both insisted they were okay after the shock of Beren finding out he had an evil twin, being thrown in jail, and Liv suffering through a coercion spell and almost marrying the wrong brother against her will.

As everyone was getting seated, Angelica took me out into the hallway and made a bubble of silence. "Lily, can you check if anyone has put any spying devices in the conference room? If you find any, kindly let me know in a subtle way."

I smiled. "Yes, Ma'am." She led the way back inside. I

drew magic from the river and pulled out my phone. *If there are any active secret spy cameras or secret listening devices in here, show me each of them being put here.*

Crap. One man had been in this room—how long ago, I couldn't tell—and he was bugging the place. In order to film everything properly while being filmed, I was going to have to pretend. "If I scan the room with my camera, we can figure out how to rearrange the furniture in a more feng shui way with that app I was telling you about. Oh, and did you like my accidental rhyme?"

Even though Angelica knew I was pretending, she still wrinkled her forehead. "We can do without the ridiculous observations, dear. We can all hear that it rhymes. We don't need you to tell us."

"Why do you have to take all the fun out of everything?" I didn't know if she was kidding or just going along with the ruse by being herself, but just in case she wasn't, I needed to get my displeasure out there.

"It's my job, or hadn't you heard?" Ah, so she *was* joking. Thank goodness.

I finished capturing the hiding spots. There were only two listening devices—one in the fake pot plant in the corner and one embedded in the frame of the chair at the head of the table. Thankfully, there were no cameras. I supposed if there were, our whole ruse with Chad would've been found out straight away since we'd kidnapped him from here.

Even though there were listening devices, we often made bubbles of silence in this room, so why weren't we doing it now? Maybe those devices could hear past it, or maybe they were inadvertently caught in the spell? The chair one was in Ma'am's personal sphere. I magicked paper and pen to myself from my room at home and wrote the question, then handed it to Ma'am.

Her magic tickled my scalp, and words appeared on the paper. Well, talk about lazy. Also, I was jealous I didn't know how to do that. *I want them to hear what we're talking about to a certain degree and think that it's business as usual. I'm also going to plant false information about Chad since 'he' cancelled their meeting this morning.*

I looked at her, smiled, and nodded. How had I not thought of that? One reason I wasn't heading up the PIB....

Angelica clapped loudly. "Okay, everyone. Let's get started." I sat at the other end of the table next to Imani, and everyone stopped chatting and looked at Angelica. She held up the piece of paper but turned it to show the blank side. Words appeared on it. *They are listening.* A warning to not only not talk about what we'd done to Chad, but also my magical abilities. Hopefully they hadn't been spying on some of our other conversations. Surely they didn't listen to all our meetings? Was my secret already out? No, it couldn't be. Chad wouldn't have been digging for information otherwise.

I let out a relieved breath, but doubt niggled. Ignoring the waves swooshing in my stomach, I focussed on what Angelica was saying—it wasn't time to worry about me right now. There was a lot more at stake.

She folded her hands together on the tabletop and looked at Will. "Thank you for sending me the evidence you uncovered. It was extremely concerning." Talk about the understatement of the year, but she was playing it for the directors, just in case, not that she would've said it any other way. She was the master of getting the job done with minimal drama.

Will gave a nod. "My pleasure. I'm at a loss though. Did any of those guys agree to talk to James?"

"When I told them we'd release them if they honestly answered one question and if they didn't, we'd find ways to keep them there indefinitely, they agreed. The fact that they'd made threats was enough for us to keep them for a while, now with all our new terrorism laws. And because they're witches, we have more reason to be careful since witches can do a lot that non-witches can't.

I sucked in a breath. "Wow, that's harsh."

Angelica gave me a "really?" look. "In any case, we asked if they were planning to kill anyone, and they both said no. James assures me they were telling the truth, so we released them. We're still keeping a detail on each of them, just in case, but we're back to square one, and we're running out of time. And, yes, I realise I sound like a cliche on a crime show, but it's where we're at."

James folded his arms and sat back in his chair. "So, we have a rough idea of the place but not who and when. What are our next steps?"

"I spoke to Agent Chad Williamson the Third early this morning. He had to rush off to an emergency case that he didn't want to overload me with, but he said I could have access to a few additional agents. He was a lot more accommodating than normal, which was a lovely surprise." Nice name placement—it was kind of like product placement… but not. I snorted at how bad my humour was and that I still found it funny. Angelica threw a stern look my way. "I'm not even going to ask, Lily. Please refrain from snorting during meetings. It's distracting." How she could say that with a straight face was beyond me.

"Yes, Ma'am." Her idea to make it sound like he was sliding to our side was also a nice touch. From what he'd said, the directors were using him to make Angelica's life hard and make the PIB look like a waste of funding. Hmm, under-mining him this way would ensure if he ever managed to meet with them again, they wouldn't trust him. Not that they couldn't get the truth out of him with a spell, but still. Although, now that we knew how to hide that spell, maybe we should use a coercion spell on Chad. We were past the point of worrying about too many legalities where the directors were concerned. All's fair in love and war, so they said, and this was definitely a war. We were all fighting for our lives and the lives of future victims.

"As I was saying, we have some extra agents we can use for surveillance. It's going to be extremely complicated, and I won't rule out putting some of them on that train."

My mouth dropped open. Imani's head jerked up straighter, and a flash of surprise broke through Will's usual meeting poker face.

Crap. I resisted the urge to take photos of everyone. How firm was she on this idea? Surely she wouldn't send everyone to die if that's what it showed on my phone. If we died, didn't it meant those we were trying to save would die, too, so what would be the point?

Will raised his hand. "Yes, Agent Blakesley."

"You know I will always follow orders, and I'm not questioning your ideas on this, but why would you want us on that train? If we can't pinpoint who it is, we're sitting ducks. They might even have planted explosives to be detonatable from outside the train. Anything is possible. I'm not sure how we can help in that situation."

"I'm going with the odds, Agent Blakesley. The same percentage of witches know how to make explosives as humans, I'm guessing. If that's the case, it means it's unlikely. Just in case, we'll sweep the train while it's at Sloane Square in the afternoon and Gloucester Road Station in the morning. I know someone there." It seemed as if Angelica knew people everywhere. "Delaying a train a few minutes is far easier than stopping it running at all. You'll also be able to keep an eye on any witch who's there. There aren't many to start with, and ones who catch public transport are rare." Our ability to travel meant we didn't have to suffer the inhumanity of sitting next to a stinky person, someone who took up most of the seat, or someone who coughed all over their fellow travellers. Yay, that this also meant this witch would stand out. "If it's a spell they're casting, you can block them the moment it happens."

Will wasn't done yet. "But won't they think it's odd if they see a few witches in their carriage? They'll be on edge as it is. We might scare them off. And if they don't act, we'll have to wait for another chance. We can't exactly decide they're guilty and take them in for questioning with no proof."

Angelica cocked her head to the side. "Why not?"

Will raised a brow. "The law. With all due respect, this is a slippery slope, Ma'am." Angelica quietly breaking the law was far different from one who decided that it wasn't applicable anymore.

"You may be excused from this case if you like, Agent Blakesley. I can assure you that if we have the wrong person, they will be released quickly. We can claim mistaken identity. I'm even happy to write them a cheque for personal suffering. Not that we're planning on roughing anyone up." She folded her arms and trained her laser-sharp gaze on him. There sure was a lot of arm folding going on today.

A lesser person would have squirmed under her fierce observation, but Will placed his elbows on the chair arms, linked his fingers together, and leaned back, as casually as you pleased. "I'm in." I wasn't sure how much of this whole meeting was honest and how much was for the directors' benefit. The pessimist in me said it really was what she planned, and the optimist was too tired from the last few months to argue. I knew just how she felt.

"Good. Our first operation happens this afternoon. I'll email the details shortly. Now, are there any questions?" She magicked a sign that said *Meeting at my place as soon as we get out of here.* "No? Excellent. Keep an eye on your inboxes, and I'll see you later. Dismissed."

Angelica nodded to me to go first. I supposed it was because I could unlock the door and let everyone in. The reception room would get ridiculously crowded otherwise. I did as asked and went straight through to the living room. We'd need more chairs than the Chesterfields, so I magicked some of the kitchen chairs into the room and sat on one.

Angelica, Mum, and Millicent sat on one Chesterfield. Beren, Liv, and James sat on the other one. Will and Imani sat on dining chairs on either side of me. Angelica cast a bubble of silence and raised a hand to ask for quiet. "Before we go any further, I am serious about getting on the train. We need bodies on every carriage to mitigate harm."

My eyes widened. "Do you have to use that word?"

Her brow wrinkled. "Which one?"

"Bodies."

She rolled her eyes. "Lily, we're going to do this in such a way that any deaths, especially of our agents, will be minimal, if not nonexistent. While it's still dangerous, they can wear protection spells. I would like that protection extended to those people on the train as well."

James and Beren shared a look. James cleared his throat. "With all due respect, Ma'am, this case is particularly dangerous. We don't have a clear target, and the site can't be secured properly. We don't have much control. I want to point out that protection spells require more power than some agents have, and I can't see how we can protect more than one or two people each, let alone ourselves, depending on what happens. If the train derails and there's a massive impact, our spells won't be all that effective, especially if the spell-caster gets knocked out." I wasn't quite sure how protection spells worked, but I figured they were something like a return to sender. You were protected until you ran out of power. Did it make a hard shell or squishy bubble around the witch? How would it protect one in case of a crash? Hmm, my initial assessment of having no idea was right, and now wasn't the time to ask. As usual, I'd have to wait till later to assuage my curiosity.

Angelica's mouth pressed into a hard line. As annoyed as she was, James made a good point, and I didn't want any of them to get hurt or die. I put up my hand. "Could we try and dissuade some people from getting on somehow? At least we'd stop a few casualties."

Will shook his head. "Do you know how crowded those carriages get in peak hour? The jam to get on is insane. There's no way we could do something to stop enough people getting on. And that's another problem—visibility, line of sight to the person we're trying to stop. It's already going to be a disaster. We don't want to make it worse. Rush hour is total chaos." He turned his gaze to Angelica. "I really wish you'd rethink this."

Her steely gaze left no guessing as to what she was thinking. "The offer still stands if you'd like to back out."

His jaw flexed. Will would never leave his comrades in the lurch, but what if I took a photo that showed they would all die? Would that change anything? Surely he wouldn't bother dying for a useless cause?

My shoulders started to ache, and my heart raced. Gah. I couldn't stay silent. I jumped up. This was way too urgent to put my hand up for. "You can't send them to their deaths. This is crazy. There must be another way." I glanced at my mother. She was biting her lip and picking at a fingernail. I wanted to beg her to let me help her get her magic back so she could use her talent at foretelling. My gut churned. But after the last time I'd tried to have that conversation, I didn't think there was any point. The last thing anyone needed right now was to watch Mum and me argue.

I looked back at Angelica and awaited her response.

"Please sit down, dear. I'm going to hurt my neck peering up at you."

I clenched and unclenched my fists, then sat. Just because I'd complied, didn't mean I'd given up. If she didn't have a good answer, I'd do what I could to stop everyone from going. Maybe the only way to do it was to tell them I was coming too. They'd hate that.

"Good. Thank you. I appreciate that you're worried, dear, but we can handle ourselves." She looked at Will, then James. "You all forget that we're probably dealing with one witch. Anyone drawing magic in one of those carriages will be an easy target. You'll be looking out with your other sight. As soon as the magic starts, you can put a return to sender up for yourselves and those around you. If it's a bomb, we'll sniff it out before the train leaves—whether they've planted it or carried it on—and arrest any witches on sight as a precaution. I'm sure that we'll have enough numbers to do this. I admit there is a risk, but it's not huge." She looked back at me. "And, Lily, of course I want you to take photos. We have a plan now.

If everyone is see through, we'll revise the plan until we come up with something that's reasonable and minimises casualties. Unfortunately, we don't have much time to muck around with things. And if the event doesn't happen today, we'll take photos and get on the train again tomorrow, and every day until the day it happens."

"Why don't we do those photos right now, then?" I couldn't just go quietly into the night. I was going to live up to my pain-in-the-bottom reputation. Without waiting for an answer, I pulled my phone out and set it to camera. As I drew my magic, everyone stopped moving. It was as if everyone, including Angelica, held their breaths.

There was so much at stake.

I pressed the red button and started recording. I began with Angelica, panning across the Chesterfield to my mother and Millicent. I wanted to sag in relief that they were as solid as ever, but I had a ways to go. I pointed my phone across to the other Chesterfield, starting with Beren. Phew. Liv was fine, too, not that she was supposed to be on that train, but still, getting that confirmation was nice.

It was as if ice cubes flowed through my veins rather than blood. Goosebumps smothered my skin, and I shivered so hard my teeth chattered. James knew. I was like a shining beacon of death.

My brother was see through.

Tears gathered at my lashes, but I couldn't fall apart now—I still had two people to scan.

I turned my phone towards Imani and Will.

My whispered word fell with my tears. "No...."

Silence.

Even Angelica had paled.

I drew my magic and willed the video to replay on the

white ceiling. I looked up, everyone's gazes following mine. We watched the replay. Millicent, even though she knew why I reacted, gasped and slammed a hand over her mouth when a near-transparent James appeared. As Imani, then Will came into shot, I looked down at them. They had discarded their poker faces, different emotions fleeting across their faces too fast for me to decipher.

When the video finished, I stared at Angelica. "Do I have to play it again?"

She cleared her throat. "No, dear. That's quite enough."

Millicent's gaze kept ping-ponging from James to Angelica —back and forth, back and forth. My mother stared at James, her knuckles white as she wrung her hands together. Fear glazed her eyes. I was sure that once she'd found words, she was going to insist he didn't go.

I turned and looked down at Will. He was looking at the floor, his breaths deep and forceful, as if he were angry at the whole situation. Just in case he needed help deciding, I said, "You can't go. You're not allowed to die." His focus returned as his head swung up and his gaze met mine, indecision clear on his face. Duty warred with the desire to survive. "Don't break my heart." I held up my hand and pointed at my engagement ring. Then I looked at Angelica. "Think of another plan. This one isn't good enough." I lifted my chin and jammed my teeth together so tears wouldn't spoil the bossy effect I was going for. Even if I ended up standing here crying, I wouldn't give in. "No one is taking away the two men I love most in this world."

Angelica cringed at that. Finally, I was getting through. And even if I wasn't, I meant what I said.

My mother sniffed. "I'm with Lily on this one." She turned to Angelica. "Think of another way. I can't abide this. I just can't."

Angelica took a deep breath and calmly looked at everyone. "Okay, James and Will can coordinate things from the van." Her gaze found me. "Film everyone again. See how that changes things."

I did as she asked. This time Will and James were fine, and I let the tears of relief wet my cheeks. But Imani was see through. Crap. I shook my head. "They're okay, but Imani isn't, and I'm not losing one of my best friends either."

Angelica stared at the ceiling and blew out a forceful breath. She brought her head down. "Right, so Imani is out. I don't have that many other agents I can call off jobs or ones who are strong enough to deal with whatever this is. We can't go into this undermanned."

No one had asked, but I thought I'd better check. I turned the phone towards Millicent. "Um, you're not going to believe this, but…."

Angelica shook her head. "Don't tell me that Millicent is see through."

"Okay, I won't."

She sighed. "Well, I'm not sure what to do. I can't not try and save all those other lives. What do all of you suggest, then? Do we sacrifice a few agents to potentially save scores of others, or do we guarantee a hundred or more deaths to save a handful of us? Whose lives are worth more?"

"Ours." I didn't hesitate. "I mean, to me, any of you mean more than a million other people. My heart breaks for the other families, but I'm not that selfless."

Will looked at me. "Lily, you're forgetting that we risk our lives all the time; we just don't have you following us around with the camera to warn us. Even you run around risking your life for things that matter. Why is this any different?"

"Because it's guaranteed. I can't live without you, or James, or Imani. James has a child, for goodness' sake. Not to mention, how will the PIB operate without its best people? If you all die, who's going to support Angelica against the directors when they try to shut it down."

Angelica swore. We all snapped our gazes to her. She never swore. She stood. "Chad. I forgot about him. He hasn't been fed since early this morning. I don't like him, but I can't torture him. Damn it. I don't have time for this."

What Will said got to me. Guilt stabbed holes into my argument. Tiny, painful doorways that my resolve seeped out of. Maybe there was a way, one last thing to try. "Ma'am, I need you to agree to something, just to see if it changes things."

Everyone stared at me, my mother's expression sinking one step further into despair. If they knew me, they likely knew what I was about to say. "What if I went too, and I was in the carriage with the most see-through people? I have a pretty good idea after all that footage I took. You just have to agree, then I can take pictures of everyone again. But you have to mean it." I met my mother's worried gaze. "And, Mum, if this doesn't work, don't worry—none of us will be there. But if none of us are going to die, then you have nothing to worry about."

She didn't look totally convinced, but she nodded. "I know you need to find a way. I'll still worry, but it won't be nearly as bad."

Angelica's steady gaze didn't waver. "Yes, of course. I think it's a good idea. You're one of the strongest witches we have. Maybe it will make the difference. I should've thought of it myself." She gave my mother a quick glance. Maybe she was trying to keep me out of as many dangerous situations as she could. Who knew what she'd promised my mother?

I swallowed and crossed my toes—I would've crossed my fingers, but I needed my hands to take the video. I started with Millicent and made my way around, holding my breath. Millicent, check. Angelica, check. James, check. Beren, check. Will, check. Imani, check. I turned the phone around to film me so I didn't have to press Stop. What would I find when I watched it back? Had my idea worked?

I flipped the phone around and pressed Stop. Then I played it back. James stood and watched over my shoulder. The video panned around the group, and then the shot spun around to the windows as I'd turned it to me.

My breath left me in a rush, and I smiled. The tears this time were of the happy variety. James grinned. "Woohoo! Lily's idea worked! We're doing this."

Will jumped up and hugged me. "Thank you, Lily."

"Would you have gone anyway?"

He stood back and looked down at me. "I honestly don't know. I do know that if I hadn't gone, those people's deaths would have haunted me forever."

Angelica stood. "You know we can't save everyone in this life, dear. We must try, though. And I agree—it would've been a terrible blow to my psyche and the PIB as a whole if we'd had to abort this mission." She smiled. "Now that's settled, I have to feed Chad and inform a few of our more powerful agents of their new assignment. We'll meet at Sloane Square and follow one of the affected retail workers. I'll have agents already through the gates at the station. James, I'll coordinate them, but you're my eyes and ears when we're down there." Her magic prickled my scalp. "I want you, Will, and Lily in the worst-affected carriage. I want each of you to wear one of these." She opened her hand to reveal three small, black bead-looking things. "There's also ones for Imani and Beren. I'd like you two to stay together as well." She turned and handed one to each of them. "They'll magically stick to your shirt collars. We'll dress for the job today, minus our jackets—it's too hot, and we don't want to stand out. In our black pants and shirts, we'll look like any other office worker or waitstaff, but when it comes to making an arrest, we'll look official."

"What about in terms of the perpetrator noticing we're all witches and getting scared off?" Will had mentioned it before, and she hadn't really answered. Unless it was going to be in the email she was supposedly sending us—I wasn't sure if that was also part of the ruse to the directors.

"Ah, yes, that." She cocked her head to the side. "I know this puts you at risk, but cut off your power so your aura isn't showing. I'll entrust Will to be the live lookout, and I can observe using those cameras you're wearing. One witch in the station won't look suspicious, and if you two indulge in some PDA, he'll assume Will's there because of his non-witch girl-friend." I had to hand it to her—she was good at thinking on her feet. "So, are we all clear?"

Millicent put up her hand. "What about me, Ma'am?"

"I'd like you to stay with me. We might need backup around or outside the station. Also, if we have any emergen-cies with that dolt in the cage, I'll need you to stand in for me and coordinate everything."

"Consider it done." Millicent smiled.

My mother stood and came over to James and me. She drew us in for a group hug. "Be careful, both of you."

James and I wrapped our arms around her and each other, and he said, "Don't worry. We'll be fine. Lily's talent's confirmed it. I just hope we can save everyone else."

"I bet you will. I have faith in both of you." She moved out of the hug and gave us both a proud smile. My chest warmed with love. This support was hard won. Maybe she was finally getting used to the idea of me being a capable adult and witch.

"Oh, Kat, can I have you liaising with Liv at headquarters? If we need additional support, we'll need you to help facilitate it, and with your knowledge of operations, it will happen faster. I'll keep a line open to you when we're on site, so you'll be speaking to either me or Agent Bianchi."

"If you want to transport Liv and me there now, we can get organised. Also, should we talk about Lily's talents in code?"

"Yes. And, of course, don't mention Chad."

Mum smiled. "Great. That doesn't seem too complicated." She looked at Liv. "Are you ready, sweetie?"

Liv nodded. "It's been good to have time to hide away by ourselves, but getting over everything that happened with Daniel will take time, and I do miss work. He does too." She gave Beren a smile.

"I do. We've binge-watched four different Netflix series. I'd prefer to be out there doing something. Liv and I don't want to let what happened affect our lives any more than it already has. And we'll both keep getting counselling as long as we need it."

James clapped Beren on the back. "We're overjoyed to have you back, mate."

"Right, then." Angelica took back control. If she let us all chat, we could be here until midnight. She looked at Mum and Liv. "Okay, you two, let's get back to headquarters; then I'll check on our little friend. James, I'll see you at four at Sloane Square. I'll email you the details, and you can organise the other agents."

"Yes, Ma'am."

Angelica made a doorway in the middle of the room and followed Mum and Liv through. Now all we had to do was wait until four o'clock. Easy-peasy lemon squeezy. Ha ha, yeah right. I chuckled.

"What's so funny?" Will asked.

"I spend too much of my life doing things I don't want to do."

His brow wrinkled. "If you don't want to work with the PIB, you can say no."

I laughed. "It's not that. It's the waiting. You know how much I hate it."

"I know how to distract you." Will smirked.

Imani squeezed her eyes shut. "Noooooo. None of that, thanks. I have a better way to distract her that we can all participate in."

I grinned. "Do tell."

"How does a chocolate muffin and coffee at Costa sound?"

"Like heaven."

Will's eyebrows rose. "Are you saying you'd rather eat at Costa?"

I gave him an innocent smile. "Yes."

He placed a hand on his heart. "Oh, how you wound me, cruel vixen."

I laughed. "I know how to fix that."

Imani chuckled. "A chocolate muffin!"

"Yes!"

"Looks like you've been outvoted, Will." James smiled. "Mill, have you got time for food?"

"Definitely. Let's do this!" She linked one arm through James's and one through Beren's. "It's a lovely day for a stroll."

And that's how we ended up at Costa, enjoying each

other's company before one of the most dangerous operations ever. None of us wanted to dwell and work ourselves into a lather of stress.

Scores, if not hundreds of people were relying on us, and they didn't even know it.

We'd better not let them down.

CHAPTER 7

Will and I held hands as we descended the stairs into the station, following three of the affected retail workers we'd found yesterday. My video showed that one of them was still going to die. But that meant we'd at least saved two. There must be a way to stop that person from getting on the train. At what point did the universe decide who was going to live and who was going to die? Had things changed as soon as we'd made the decision to intervene and get on the train? Or were there still things that could only be decided in the moment? And if the event didn't happen today, would who was going to die stay the same? Thousands of ants swarmed my belly as my overwrought nerves fired up—I hoped whatever it was, was happening today. I'd be an absolute wreck if I had two more weeks of morning and afternoon trips to a potential massacre.

I flicked my phone towards Will, just in case anything had changed. He was still fine, thank God.

"Time to block your powers, Lily. You shouldn't be doing

that."

"I know. It's become a compulsion. I just want to make sure."

"Well, don't. You'll mess it all up if our target gets suspicious."

I slid my phone into my pocket and blocked my access to the river. It was like turning the heater off after sitting in front of it. The inner warmth I'd taken for granted disappeared, and I was left feeling empty and cold, even in the heat of the summer afternoon.

It was five after five. Streams of people jostled us as we all flowed onto the platform. I looked around, trying to be subtle. Not that I had my magic activated, but whoever this was, was probably going to be acting a bit sus. If I saw anyone that set my spidey sense to pinging, I'd let Will know.

I spotted James, who was waiting down the platform, in front of where we had figured the worst-hit carriage would be. The one guy who was see through split from his friends. He stopped near James, and the workmates kept walking. Right. That proved it.

I wanted so much to grab my phone and light up my aura like a Christmas tree so I could see who was still going to die. Instead of pulling out my phone, I chewed on a fingernail. Thankfully, Will was too busy looking out for our bad guy to notice and tell me to stop.

I lowered my voice, but I couldn't make a bubble of silence —not that we needed one in all the noise. A train appeared from the tunnel, going the opposite way. It pulled up at the platform across from us, brakes screeching. I cringed and waited for the station person's address to finish before I spoke to him. "See any you know whats yet?"

"No. Just Imani and B waiting near the next carriage from

the one we're getting on." He gave a brief nod. "There are four other agents down there."

Looked like they were covering four carriages. What was supposed to happen to the people in other carriages? Did the PIB have that few in the way of powerful agents? Maybe they were otherwise indisposed. This operation was short notice. There was a chance it wouldn't happen today. Would extra planning time enable us to get our act together so no one ended up dying?

Will squeezed my hand. "There and there."

"What? There are two?"

"Yes. That guy in the black T-shirt and jeans. He just stood next to James."

"Crap. Who's the other one?"

"That man with the beard and red cap."

"He's two carriages down. Do you think they're working together?"

"I can't see any interaction between them, but who knows?"

Will briefly touched the earpiece Angelica had asked him to wear at the last minute. James and Imani had them too. I wasn't important enough to need one, apparently. I wasn't bitter about it… much. The movies made it look so cool. "Yes, Ma'am. Can you see?"

Will frowned. It's likely that whatever she said was lost in the high-pitched whine of brakes as our train arrived.

Showtime.

Will gripped my hand and pulled me towards the open doors. James and our target had ducked in just before us. It was Will's job to watch the witch and give the signal when he drew power. Once he did that, we were all to open our portals to the river, ready to cast whatever spell was required. We needed just enough time that Will could work out what spell he was invoking. It was beyond frustrating that we couldn't arrest him before he acted—we had no proof he was going to do anything.

And what if he wasn't? What if we'd gotten it wrong and today wasn't even the day?

Hopefully Beren and Imani were having better luck in the carriage with the other witch. Beren had been given permission to drop his shield if the witch was in their carriage. Hopefully he just stayed out of the guy's line of sight when he did that.

We stood across the carriage but on a diagonal to our target. Will turned his head to look around. He frowned. "What the hell is *he* doing here?"

I peered in the direction he was. "I've seen him around the PIB. Angelica's obviously giving you more backup."

"He's in the wrong carriage, for God's sake. If he stuffs this up...." Will growled. It was kind of sexy. He shook his head, then looked back at the suspected terrorist.

I bit my lip against the urge to open my portal. I tried not to stare at the man—I didn't want him to get suspicious, but it was impossible. How else would I be ready to act when the time came? At least he might not notice me in the mass of commuters.

Was he our crim? He looked to be in his twenties, dark, short-cropped hair. Stubble dirtied his fair skin. His brown eyes roved the carriage. My heart raced, and I looked away before he caught my gaze.

If he was our terrorist, why was he doing this? Was it religious, personal, or were voices telling him to? Was he acting alone, or was the witch in the next carriage part of it?

Too many questions we could never know until it was over.

One advantage we did have: if it didn't go down this evening, we could follow the men home and check them out.

The train jerked as it pulled out of the station, and I stumbled into the woman behind me. "Sorry." She looked at me but said nothing. Okay, then. If only I could take my apology back. I hated people who didn't bother to acknowledge an apology. Sheesh. How much effort did it take? *Okay, Lily, don't get distracted.*

As the train picked up speed, so did my heart rate. I looked around the carriage at all the people. How many could I protect?

Will squeezed my hand. I shot my gaze to the man as he looked over and down at someone I couldn't see through the crowd. Whoever it was, was seated. Will bent and said, "Open yourself. His aura is brightening."

My cheeks flushed as I opened to the river.

This was it. Or was it? Maybe he was going to magic a bunch of flowers into being?

Actually, he probably wasn't. His magic vibrated against my scalp. Strength, violence, and anger washed over me, and I swayed. What was he doing? I'd better warn Will. And James was standing right near him. "He's drawing a lot of power, and he's not happy."

Will's eyes widened. He spoke quietly into his earpiece, giving everyone the heads-up. Hopefully James could see what the spell was since he was the closest to the guy. We'd need James as a witness later.

My stomach clenched as the power built. What was he going to do?

A shield appeared around him, but that wasn't enough for any of us to act.

Will released my hand. I stood like a gunslinger, feet

braced, hands ready to draw… or, rather, throw magic. James edged closer to the guy. He was within two feet of him, one lady in between them. He was almost close enough to slap handcuffs on him. That would be ideal if we could cause as little fuss as possible, and handcuffs looked more legit than a guy freezing with arms jammed by his sides. We still had to be mindful of the non-witches. Mind-wiping this number of people wouldn't be impossible, but what a task to detain them all while we did it.

It was as if the oxygen was sucked out of the carriage. I gasped and struggled to breathe. Silver lines of what looked like electricity sparked down the man's shield. I only just registered the prickle of James's magic through the force of the guy we were about to arrest.

I created a bubble of protection around myself and everyone within a four-foot radius—it was all I could manage. My blood heated as I sucked magic from the river of power.

The man called out in an aggressive yet satisfied voice, "Hey, Mia, I told you, you'd regret it."

Warmth built around us, and fire exploded from the guy as James, wearing his own bubble of protection, lunged and slapped handcuffs on one of his wrists. The fire extinguished, and I could breathe again.

A woman in the carriage asked, "What was that? Did anyone see that?" Others responded in the affirmative, but no one could work it out. By then, James had the other handcuff on the guy.

Had he just stopped us all from being blown up?

My shoulders sagged in relief, and I dropped my spell. Will blew out a breath and spoke into his comms. "We have the suspect handcuffed. Ready to disembark at Kensington South." He looked at me. "Are you all right?"

I shrugged. "It was a lot of build up to nothing, thank God. I'm fine. Go do your thing. Oh, and don't forget to grab Mia, whoever she is."

Will gave me a sarcastic "no, really?" look, before making his way over to James and the other agent, who'd gotten there first.

Then everything went to hell.

The agent who wasn't supposed to be there—a six-foot-six hulk of a guy—shoved James out of the way, made a doorway, slicing two innocent commuters in half, then grabbed our suspect and pushed him through it, following before they both disappeared.

What in the seven levels of hell? I gaped.

Shrieking and shouting erupted as the train slowed to pull into the next station. James stood wide-eyed. Will swore. Men and women, blood and gore staining their clothes and dripping from their skin, clambered to move away from the carnage. I was pushed back into someone's legs who was sitting down. I struggled to stay standing and not end up in their lap.

"I'm sorry," I said to the seated woman, but she didn't hear me over the pandemonium. I gave up and tried to push through the throng. I could just see the bodies from where I was, and it wasn't pleasant. One of the victims was the man I'd seen today who was still see through. Damn it. This time I knew without a doubt my intended recipient wouldn't hear me, but it didn't matter. The word seeded in my bruised heart and dredged up through my throat. It fell from my mouth, heavy with regret and sorrow. "Sorry."

Will's magic tingled my scalp, and he called out, "Everyone, calm down and get out of the train in a slow and orderly manner. Wait on the platform for me to speak to you before you leave." A sense of peace washed over me, and I turned to leave the train with the flock. Will grabbed my arm. "Not you, Lily. Sorry. I should've warned you." He mumbled something, and the desire to serenely alight disappeared. My heart hammered again, and I was sure my armpits were a sweaty shambles of shock and horror. The pungent odour of heated bodies souring my nostrils was evidence I wasn't alone. The sooner we got out of this stinking bloodbath, the better.

An English-accented female voice came over the loudspeaker in the station. "The Circle Line train on platform one is terminating. Please vacate the train." Angelica wasn't kidding when she said she had clout, not that someone wouldn't have noticed two severed bodies on the train and made the same decision.

What a mess, and in more ways than one.

I got closer to Will and James, but not too close because I didn't want to step in anything. I frowned. That young man and a middle-aged woman were our casualties. Yes, it could've been so, so much worse, but as far as these two and their families and friends were concerned, this was bad enough. I knew we hadn't failed entirely, but why did it feel like we had?

Oh, that's right, because one of our agents took the guy God knew where. Had he gotten overzealous and taken him to headquarters? Surely not. He'd risked too much by making a doorway in front of non-witches and killing two of them. Or had he gone mad, a past case he'd worked on setting off PTSD?

I interrupted whatever James was saying to Will. "Um, that agent, has he taken the guy to jail?"

Will shook his head. "Your mum's just notified us that he's not there."

"Oh, crap." There wasn't much else I could say.

James raised a brow. "That's the understatement of the year." He shook his head. "Let's get you out of here, Lily. We need to get our forensics team in here and deal with that lot."

"Yes, and quickly." Angelica entered the carriage and surveyed the crime scene. She looked up at Will and James. "Nice work, gentlemen." She turned and looked at me. "And Lily."

"Thanks. I hardly did anything." I didn't want to take credit where it wasn't due. James had been the real hero.

"So, he was going to burn everyone to death and explode the carriage?"

"Yes, Ma'am." My brother rubbed the back of his neck. "It would've been a massive disaster. It's unfortunate that we've had two casualties, but under the circumstances…."

"Agreed." She looked at Will. "Who was the agent?"

"Craft. I wondered why the hell he was in with us in the first place, but I never could've guessed he would sabotage everything on purpose."

"Has he turned up yet?" my brother asked.

"No, and I don't expect him to. I don't know how he fits into all this, but we have a ton of work to do, so let's not waste time."

"Yes, Ma'am." Will glanced past Ma'am and out to the platform. "I have a lot of witnesses to interview. They won't leave here until they've spoken to me."

She nodded. "Understood."

Imani entered the carriage and took in the gore. "Oh, that's not good. What can I do?"

Will made his way to her at the door. "You can help me with these interviews. We want to interview a Mia in particular. Our guy yelled out to her before he tried to ignite us."

"Okay. Let's go."

Angelica turned to me. "You can make a doorway from here. We're going to have to mind-wipe everyone anyway, or at least alter their memories. We'll make them think someone had a heart attack and died on the train. It won't be that much of a stretch to wipe any memory of you disappearing."

"Okay, thanks. Good luck."

"Thank you, dear. Stay home and wait for my instructions. I think we'll need to have a meeting later."

I nodded. "Okay. Bye." I shrugged off the guilt and paranoia seeping over me at creating such an obvious spell in public, made my doorway, and stepped through.

This was not how things were supposed to have gone. Why did Agent Craft snatch him away? Was he in cahoots, and if he wasn't, why would he do that? And most importantly, could we track them down before another tragedy unfolded?

I unlocked the reception-room door to a waiting Abby. "Hello, gorgeous." I bent and picked her up.

You need a cuddle?

"Yes. We failed a couple of people today, and I'm sad." My throat burned as tears formed.

She purred and rubbed her face against mine. *Don't be sad. You tried your best, and no one can ask more than that.*

But we hadn't done our best. If we had, the guy would be in a cell right now.

Something had gone very wrong with one of our agents, and I had the feeling when we found out what it was, things were going to get a whole lot worse.

I squeezed Abby and longed for my childhood days, before my parents went missing, when a hug could fix almost anything. I desperately wanted those days back.

Except, they were gone forever.

CHAPTER 8

I checked the time on my phone and yawned. "It's after eleven. I think I'll go to bed." I didn't really want to sleep because of the nightmares I was sure to have—seeing two people murdered so violently wasn't something you forgot in a hurry if ever—but I was weary, both body and soul. Maybe I'd ask Angelica to give me a mindwipe when this was all over.

Abby purred. *Okay. I'll come with you.* I smiled, turned off the TV, and stood from the couch. I'd been waiting all night for Will or Angelica to contact me, but they must've been too busy. Surely any meeting could now wait until tomorrow.

I turned off the light and crossed the hallway to the stairs. My phone dinged, and I jumped. "Oh, God. Seriously. Why is everyone always trying to kill me?" Abby meowed, and it sounded suspiciously like laughter.

I looked at my phone. It was a message from Will. *Heads-up. We're all coming back now for a meeting. Make sure you're decent.* Hopefully tracksuit pants and T-shirt were decent. And I was wearing a bra. That should be enough to keep everyone happy. I turned around and opened the reception-room door, ready to draw my magic in case someone I didn't expect came through. After being kidnapped the other week, I wasn't taking any chances.

Will was the first to come through. As soon as he saw me, he smiled. His large stride took no time to reach me. His arms came around me, squishing me into his chest. "I've missed you."

"I saw you late this afternoon."

"Yeah, and it's now almost midnight. I don't usually do this, but after witnessing what went down in that train, I'm just counting my blessings. You know?"

I tilted my face up and kissed his lips. "Yes, I do know. Come on. Let's get out of the way before everyone else comes in." We moved to the living room. This time, Will ignored the dining chairs I'd magicked there for our last meeting. He dropped onto one of the Chesterfields and pulled me with him to sit on his lap. Abby had followed us and jumped up to sit in my lap. A *click, click* on the floor heralded Ted's arrival. He wagged his tail, and I patted him. When that was done, he sat at Will's feet. Well, this was cosy.

"I love my little family." Will kissed the top of my head and gave Abby a pat.

"And we love you."

"*Meow.*"

"*Woof.*"

"Hey, loves." Imani came in and sat next to me. "I'm bloody exhausted." Her head drooped forward, and she shut her eyes.

I frowned. "Did you find out anything from that woman, the one he called out to?"

"She's his ex." Will's grip on my waist tightened. "Scumbag. He's been threatening her since they broke up three months ago. She started dating someone last week, which is what we think triggered him to act."

James, Mum, Beren, Liv, and Angelica came in.

I looked past them, but no one else came through the door. "Where's Millicent?"

"She's gone home to relieve her parents from babysitting duty. She needs her sleep too. Annabelle's been waking twice at night, the last couple of nights. She's probably having a growth spurt or something and is extra hungry. I'll update her tomorrow." James sat on one of the dining chairs, as did Beren. Liv, Mum, and Angelica took the more comfortable Chesterfield.

Will tapped my thigh. "My leg's going to sleep. I think you'll have to hop off."

"Are you saying I'm too heavy?" I raised a brow and tried not to smile.

His eyes widened, horror jumping from them. "Ah… no, of course not."

I chuckled. "Just joshing. I couldn't resist." I kissed his cheek and gently pushed Imani's arm so she'd move over. I slid into the gap. "Thanks."

"My pleasure, love." She leaned towards me.

"What are you doing?"

"The couch is dipping so low under your weight, I'm falling towards you." She smirked.

"Ha, ha, ha."

Fatigue muted Angelica's voice. "If we can get started, that would be great. I'm ready for bed. It's been a reticulated python kind of a day." Trust her to come up with a snake analogy. She could've come up with something nice to compare the length to—I couldn't think what, but surely there was something. A conga line of squirrels maybe?

Mum laughed. "Ridiculously long?"

"Yes." Angelica tilted her head side to side, stretching her neck. Once she'd done that, she spoke. "For Lily's benefit, I'll begin at the beginning. Our first suspect, the man who tried to blow up the train, is Matthew Larson. He left the military with PTSD a year ago. While he was there, he was a bomb specialist. I would imagine he used magic to help him get ahead because there was nothing unmagical about how he tried to blow up that train."

"And that agent? What's his deal?" I hadn't had much time to think about it—witnessing what happened to those victims... well, I was still processing.

Angelica's magic tingled my scalp, and a folder appeared in her hand. She opened it and read. "Agent Paul Craft, twenty-eight, recruited seven years ago. An only child who lost his father when he was fifteen. Associated with petty criminals at senior school but cleaned up his act and joined the bureau. Has a spotless record other than the friends he kept, who he no longer associates with. He's been a good agent, put away many dangerous criminals. Before today, I would say I had nothing but praise for him." She placed the folder on the low table between Chesterfields. "Feel free to look through his file if you like. It gives his personality profile, strengths and weaknesses, etc. Maybe you can figure it out. At this stage, we have no clear idea as to why, but I've asked your brother to do a deeper dive into his life outside of work."

"Could he have snapped or panicked?" I asked.

She shrugged. "Possibly snapped, but not panicked. Agents don't panic, dear. It's been trained out of them, if it was indeed part of their make-up in the first place. You've heard of fight or flight? We choose people who have the fight tendency. We hone them so they choose a logical action rather than a shoot-now-and-ask-questions-later reaction—he knows our processes and procedures and could probably do them in his sleep. We'll look into whether he wanted to mete out his own justice. But that's a big choice—he's forfeiting his job, reputation, and, when we catch up to him, his freedom."

"Is he the new boyfriend of the intended victim?"

Will shook his head. "We got those details from the woman at the station. Her new boyfriend is a non-witch—as is she. We asked her subtle questions and deduced she didn't know Matthew was a witch. She has no idea we exist. We found her new boyfriend and asked him a few questions—he was leaving his job twenty miles away at the time of the disaster. We briefly interviewed him, but it was only to confirm he wasn't our guy, and he obviously wasn't."

Angelica turned to my mother. "Did you put out the bulletins for both Matthew and Agent Craft?"

"Yes. All our agents are aware of it, including our overseas branches."

Angelica stood. "We've had agents visit both men's homes with no luck. We've stationed two agents inside each home. We can't do much else tonight, and we all need sleep after today's horrors. We won't dither tomorrow, though. Everyone, meet back here tomorrow morning at eight." She walked to the door and turned around. "Thank you for your exceptional work today." She exited, the stairs creaking once as she trod on the third stair on the way up to her room.

We all said our goodbyes, and Will and I headed up to bed, Abby racing up the stairs in front of us. At least we were all safe and accounted for and none of us were being targeted by anyone. I should enjoy that while I could because reprieves never lasted long.

❧

I sat on a dining chair in our morning meeting, rubbing my eyes and trying hard to focus. The nightmares hadn't held back. I'd relived the moment Agent Craft's doorway killed those two poor people. A thought hit me, and I woke up all the way pretty quickly. I put up my hand.

"Yes, Lily." Angelica was back to her usual poker-faced self.

"You mindwiped all those commuters and planted a fake memory of a heart attack victim. How did you explain what happened to the families of the deceased? Like, how did you explain them being chopped in two? What kind of accident has that outcome?"

"Our expert morticians. Two of them worked all night to put those bodies back together and make it look like a heart attack. There won't be any news reports, and as far as the families know, their loved one was the only one who died."

"But you can still charge him with murder, even if the families don't know that's what happened?" This was so confusing. Who would ask for justice if they didn't know they needed to?

She gave me a look as if I'd just lost half my IQ. "Of course, dear. We don't normally cover things up to this extent, but because magic was involved and it would be impossible to give it another spin people would believe, we've had to resort to subterfuge. The outcome will be the same—the person will be grieved, and we'll do our best to ensure justice is served."

Imani nodded. "And, to some extent, this is better for those left behind. Less-violent deaths are easier to absorb. They'll still be devastated—the victims were so young—but the way they died won't be something the loved ones will have nightmares about."

I considered it. "I suppose you're right." I believed in honesty at all costs, but this proved that in some instances, I was wrong. Why make people suffer for nothing when the outcome was ultimately the same? "So now what do we do? How do we find a pigmy possum in a national park?"

Angelica stared at me for a beat too long. "Do you always have to be *different*, dear?"

I smiled. "Yes. I don't mind a cliché every now and then, but there's nothing wrong with cutening something up when one has the opportunity."

She raised a brow. "Cutening?" She shook her head. "All right. Time to focus." She smoothed a hand over her immaculate bun. "There's been no sightings of the pair. Our agents have had time to go through Agent Craft's belongings at his home to look for any clues, and they've found nothing out of the ordinary." She looked at me. "It's time to employ some other methods. Would you mind taking some pictures at headquarters? If we find nothing there, we'll go to his place. We need to figure this out as quickly as possible. We have no idea what he's done with our other suspect, and if he plans on letting him go, we're in even more trouble, both with potential danger to the public and his ex, and it will give the directors another black mark to use against us when they talk the powers that be out of funding us." She moved her gaze to James. "If we can get a clearer picture from Lily's photos, we can plan further. But until then, I think you all need to work on your other existing cases, but be ready to go, go, go. If we have nothing to work with after Lily does her thing, we'll reconvene and brainstorm."

James gave a nod. "Yes, Ma'am."

Angelica looked at Mum and Will. "You can both come with Lily and me. After this, I have to go check on our other little project." Ah, Chadiot. I'd almost forgotten about him. We couldn't keep him captive forever. How long did we have until the directors figured it out? I shivered at the prospect. "See you all later. You know what to do." She made her doorway in the middle of the room and left.

I looked at Mum and smiled. "You can come with me."

She smiled back. "Thank you, sweetie."

I bade goodbye to everyone else and made my portal, then followed Mum through. Will came in after me as Angelica chatted to Gus at the door. When he saw us, Gus gave us his usual cheery greeting.

"Hey, Gus. How's everything?" Doh! I needed to think before I spoke. If I ended up having to listen to something gross, I only had myself to blame. Dammit!

"Well, Miss Lily, my wife has to go in for bunion surgery."

Argh, feet. One of my least-favourite topics. "Oh, that's not good."

"I'd love to chitchat, but we have work to do. Please excuse us." Angelica turned to Mum, Will, and me. Come on." She gave Gus a poker-faced look. "Have a productive day." I almost laughed. A normal person would say to have a lovely day, but being productive was more important to Angelica than someone being happy.

I gave Gus a small wave as we walked past him, but for once, I wasn't sorry that Angelica was abrupt. I'd have to thank her later. If only I didn't worry so much about upsetting people, I'd be more like her and less like me. Sometimes, when I was nice to others, it was at the expense of my own comfort. There were circumstances where I wouldn't change that, but there were instances where I should stick up for myself more. I'd have to work on that.

We strode to the elevator, then made our way to Angelica's office. Once in there, Angelica made a bubble of silence. "I've checked for bugs, and we're clear, but I'd like you to confirm something else for me, please, Lily. A while ago, I suspected someone had been through my drawers. I have spells on them to stop others opening them and to act as an alarm that sounds on my phone. I didn't receive the alarm, but I just have a sixth sense that they've been tampered with. Can you please take some photos for me?"

"Of course I can." I pulled out my phone, brought up the camera app, and drew from the river of power. "Show me anyone who has been in here tampering with Angelica's drawers." Hmm, that could be considered rude, but I was thinking about her table drawers rather than her underwear. I couldn't help the chuckle that erupted.

Will shook his head. "I can't see what's so funny about this. You can't see a squirrel in here, can you?"

"Ha ha, no. Besides, squirrels don't tamper. They're too sweet and cute. I told you we should start recruiting them. You're missing out on a massive opportunity."

Angelica cocked her head to the side. "I did think you were being ridiculous, but they helped you enormously with overcoming Daniel and saving Olivia. Maybe we'll look into it when this is all over." Whether she meant this case or our beef with the directors, who knew?

I looked down at my phone screen and gasped. "Crap." I took a photo of a man going through her middle drawer—I could assume he'd gone through the others too. His top hat was a dead giveaway. "It's Brosnan." I handed the phone to

Angelica. Will and Mum stood on either side of her and peered at it.

"I knew it." Angelica pressed her lips together. "No doubt, he was looking for something to incriminate me. I've never trusted him. He's always been a misogynistic faecal smear." My mouth dropped open, and Will choked. Angelica held her head high. "What? I'm allowed to swear, too, you know."

I nodded. "Of course you are. I've just hardly ever heard you before, and as far as swearing goes, that's fairly polite and inventive. If I were scoring you, I'd give you a ten out of ten." I smiled.

She allowed her lips to curve up. "Why, thank you, dear." It didn't take her long to frown again. "Can you find out when?"

"I think so." I held my phone up and asked my magic if he was last here in January. He didn't show up until I got to April.

"Thank you, dear. So, when I was in hiding for a while." I would've asked her why she was in hiding—had they threatened her outright, and if they had, how could she come back—but she was unlikely to tell me, and it was irrelevant right now. We had other things to worry about. "Sit."

Mum and I sat on the guest chairs, and Will magicked another one in from Ma'am's outer office and sat. He looked at Angelica. "Would he have found anything?"

"Of course not, dear. There was nothing to find except case files of whatever I was working on, and my work-contacts list."

Mum bit her lip, maybe deciding whether to ask a question or not. Yes won out. "What were they looking for?" She glanced at Will and me, then directed her gaze back to Angelica. "You know you can trust them. I'm sure we'd all be happy to swear to silence. We're here to support you."

Something flashed in her gaze, but it was gone before I could get a read on what it was. Was she grateful or annoyed? She gave my mother a gentle smile. "I appreciate it, Kat, but the less everyone knows, the better. I have no doubt that you'll all support me in any situation, but in this case, I don't need it… yet. If there is a time where you need to know, rest assured, I'll spill the proverbial beans."

"Okay, but I just wanted you to know."

"I know." She took a deep breath and sat up straighter. "Right, back to the case. The first stop will obviously be Agent Craft's office. After that, a visit to Chad's office is in order."

"What about the office protection spells and his bulldog of an assistant?" Will asked.

"Chad emailed her an order that stated I was in charge in his absence, and I backed that up with his verbal communication on the phone before that spell ran out. Under duress, I made him call her this morning to say he had something urgent to attend to and wouldn't be back for a couple of days." That wasn't super imaginative.

"Um, won't she get suspicious when he doesn't come back?"

"Maybe we'll figure out a way to have him here but under our control before it comes to that. We could potentially have him here for short periods with Agent Lavender Belrose hiding a control spell in his aura. The energy it will take means we're limited to a couple of hours here and there, and Agent Belrose would have to be in the building the entire time Chad is here. In any case, we'll worry about that when it happens. As for his assistant, Muriel, what do you propose? I'm open to suggestions." Angelica always had a plan up her sleeve. Was she testing us, or did she not like her own plan very much?

Will crossed his legs, putting his ankle up to rest on his

other knee. "Get Liv to have lunch with her. From what I've heard, she likes her. Remember we had Liv befriend her for information, hmm, unless that was when you weren't here."

"I seem to recall something—even if I wasn't here, I had ears out." She gave him a "you should know better" look. "That's a simple and effective solution." She grabbed her phone. "Hello, Olivia. I have a favour to ask." The call lasted a couple of minutes. Angelica hung up. "She's good to go. She'll text me to let me know when they're down in the eatery."

"What if Muriel doesn't want to go to lunch today?" The woman was a witch, so it wasn't like anyone could cast a spell on her to make her say yes without her knowing.

Angelica smiled. "Olivia's going to give her a sob story and ask for advice. Muriel is a bulldog, as Will so subtly pointed out earlier, but she has a good heart. I don't think she'll be able to say no."

Mum said, "We have plenty of time, then. Shall we start with Craft's office now anyway? Lily can always go home for a bit and come back at lunch? Besides, you never know what Lily will uncover that we have to chase up."

Angelica nodded. "True. Okay, then, people." She stood and led the way from her office to Agent Craft's. His was, apparently, down one level and at the opposite end of the complex to Angelica's office. When we got there, Angelica frowned, then shared an irritated look with Will.

"What's wrong?" Mum asked.

Will narrowed his eyes at the door. "It's magically locked. If you use your other sight and think about the handle and opening the door, you'll see." Sadness darkened Mum's eyes, and Will's face fell. "I'm so sorry, Katerina. I didn't think."

She shook her head. "It's okay. I'm used to it now. Don't worry."

Even if she didn't want it, I gave her a quick hug. When I was sure she was okay, I did what Will had suggested and drew a small amount of power. The door handle and frame of the door glowed blue. A line ran through the glow with blips every now and then, kind of like a heart-monitor readout. "What are the blippy things?"

"It's an alarm. It's set to the rhythm of the siren. If we open that door without disarming it, Gus, or whoever else is on security on this floor at the time, will come running to investigate. Agent Craft will also be notified, likely by an app on his phone. It will give us an electric shock if we try to disarm it without the passcode."

I shook my head. "Magic blows my mind. How you link it to technology is freaky."

Mum patted my arm. "I'm still trying to catch up with all the new magical advancements. Angelica's been educating me." Sadness crept back into her eyes. "Except I'll never experience it firsthand."

I wanted to tell her that she was wrong, that I could help her, but I bit my tongue. Once bitten twice shy—it was better if I bit myself rather than get chewed out by my mother. Plus, I didn't want her to feel worse than she already did.

I tilted my head to the side. "Does it even matter if you set it off? Everyone must know by now that he's on the PIB blacklist. It makes sense that you'd go to his office."

Angelica shook her head, disappointment on her face. The disbelief in her tone was clear. "You've really missed the point... again. We're not a bunch of amateurs, dear. We don't set off alarms we should notice and know how to get past."

"But you said it had a passcode. How are you supposed to guess that?" I knew Angelica was smart and filled with agent skills, but surely she hadn't developed hacking prowess in the last few months… or had she?

Will smirked and made a bubble of silence. "That's where I come in. A couple of years ago, I developed a spell that can decode practically anything. The energy I'll use depends on the intricacy of the spell. There are some systems, like those set up to protect highly classified PIB information, that would take more energy than I had to crack—you can only ever do it in one prolonged spell. If you stop the spell to rest, you have to start from scratch, but if I had your help, for instance, I'd be able to do it." He stared at the wall for a moment, then came back to me. "Gee, Lily, your magic really does change the game. If you could link me to yourself, James, B, etc, I could probably hack into anything."

Angelica smiled. "Hmm, we'll have to hold onto that information for another time, but it's very interesting. For now, though, can you just get us into this so we can do what we need to?"

Will wore a thoughtful and excited expression. "Of course. This will take a minute." His magic prickled my scalp as he stared at the door. He held a finger up and moved it as if tracing an uneven line. He concentrated and mumbled and wiggled his finger. It actually took a bit longer than a minute, but, finally, he was done. "We're good to go." He grabbed the knob, and I cringed, waiting for the deafening blare, my hands hovering near my ears.

He turned the knob.

The door opened… silently. Success! Not that I doubted him. Ahem.

He raised a brow. "Your belief in me is amazing."

I shrugged. "Sorry. You can't override base instincts sometimes."

He shook his head and led the way through to Craft's office. He had the outer office, which held an empty receptionist desk, chair, and plastic plant. It was like walking into most of the other offices in the building.

Will frowned. "Sorry, but you'll have to wait a moment longer."

I engaged my other sight and concentrated on the shut door to his office. This spell looked more intricate than the other one. I wasn't even going to ask. Will said he was the best, and this time, I was happy to believe him. I checked the time on my phone to see how long it would take. Twelve minutes later, his magic stopped flowing, and sweat glittered on his forehead. "Done. That one was spelled with enough power to give whoever opened it a heart attack."

Angelica frowned. "He shouldn't have to do that. Any super-secret files can be stored with an encryption in our database."

My mother tapped her chin. "Unless they were super secret from you or Chad."

Angelica didn't need to answer verbally—her pinched lips were enough. She threw up a return to sender and flung the door open. She strode inside—a woman on a mission. When she reached the other side of his desk and looked at his drawers, she slammed her hands on her hips and growled. Will and I looked at each other. Oh, boy, I'd never seen her this mad. She looked at us. "He's spelled his goddamn drawers shut."

Will started walking towards. "I can dea—"

She put her hand up. "No. I'll deal with this one. Stand back."

Oh, crap.

The three of us stood at the door, and Angelica moved

back to the wall. I put a protection spell around my mother and me. "I've got you, Mum."

Her expression was resigned. "Thank you."

My scalp tingled as Angelica put on her own protection spell, then said something else. The pressure in the room built. *Bang! Crack!* The four drawers—two on either side of the desk—flew out of their homes and smashed into the wall, one splintering when it hit the rendered brick wall. The table legs split into pieces, and the whole thing slammed into the ground. Strands of electricity shot in all directions from the wreckage, stinging me as they hit my shield. The smell of ozone permeated the air. Then it was gone.

Angelica dusted her hands together as if she'd just finished a carpentry project and gave a nod. "There. That's better. It's safe to drop your spells now."

Will and Mum hurried over and joined Angelica, rifling through the debris. I held my phone up. "What exactly am I looking for?"

Angelica answered without looking up from her ferreting. "Documents that aren't to do with existing cases, meetings with Chad, that sort of thing."

"Okay." I drew magic. "Show me the last lot of documents Agent Craft wanted to keep secret from Ma'am." The table on my phone screen was intact. Chad lay back in Agent Craft's chair with his feet on the desk and his mouth open, probably in the middle of saying something dumb. So typical. I couldn't help rolling my eyes. Damn idiot.

Agent Craft stood to the side of the table, hands by his sides, an interested look and the hint of a smile on his face. What was Chad telling him? *Click.* I moved closer to the table, careful not to trip over the real-world aftermath of Angelica's frustration.

I focussed on one piece of paper on the desk—there were more pieces under it, but they might remain covered if my magic didn't choose to show them to me. I would have to ask in a minute, but for now, I pressed the button and took a picture. "Show me more of those papers." The scene changed. Chad's mouth was closed. Craft was leaning over the desk, pen in hand. I zoomed in. He was signing his name. *Click.* There was an empty space under it for director Brosnan's signature. Interesting.

"Show me another page of this contract or agreement." I wasn't quite sure what it was as I hadn't read the first page before, and I didn't want my magic to misinterpret anything. It was probably fine, but you never knew. The scene changed, and another page appeared. I took a shot and asked again. Nothing. Hopefully that would be enough to figure it out.

"Show me another document Agent Craft didn't want Angelica to see." His laptop appeared on the table. Gah. This would be tricky. I almost reached across the table to turn it around, then remembered it wasn't real... at least not in the here and now. I lowered my camera and plotted my movement. I shook my head. There wasn't anywhere I could get to that information without walking across the decimated table-top. Oh, well. I placed one foot on it to test it. Hmm, it seemed stable enough. What the hell. Might as well. Ha, that rhymed. I giggled. No one bothered asking, which suited me fine. It was annoying when you couldn't have a private joke with yourself without everyone wanting to know why you were laughing. Today, I would take my good fortune and enjoy it.

I made it to the other side and held my phone up again. "Show me that last document again." The intact table and laptop appeared. I focussed on the screen and took a photo.

"Show me more." Nothing happened. Seriously? "Why do you have to leave me in suspense?"

Will looked up. "What's wrong?"

"There's more to see, but the powers that be won't show me." Oh my God, I was on fire with the rhyming today. Shame there wasn't a medal for this stuff. It was also a shame that I was the only person who appreciated it.

"Can I see?"

"Not yet. I'll take the rest of the photos first; then we can go through them all. It'll be less confusing. Plus, we don't want anyone else in here seeing what I do."

"Fair enough." He picked something out of the disaster and added it to a pile.

My mother sat back. "Why aren't you just lifting it all with your magic and asking the papers we need to just slip out?"

Angelica shook her head. "I don't want to draw more attention to us. We're lucky that me making this mess didn't have security running down here. I know Gus can stall for us once, but twice…. It's one thing for everyone to know we're investigating that agent, but it's another for them to know Lily and you are helping. I don't want to draw unnecessary attention to either of you. We don't know what Craft is mixed up in. The fewer targets plastered on people's backs, the better."

Mum nodded and went back to digging through the wreckage while I made my way to the door and lifted my phone. I turned towards where the desk used to be. Well, it *was* still there but not in the same format. "Show me the last meeting Craft had that he wanted to keep secret from Ma'am."

A man stood on the other side of Craft's desk, hands on hips. He wore an agent's uniform and black-framed glasses. His black hair, parted on the side with a fringe over one eye, reached his jaw. It was very rock and roll or emo, and I wouldn't have been surprised to find he was wearing eyeliner. I had no idea who the man was, but there was something familiar about him. Craft was on this side of the table, sitting in a chair, his back to me. It seemed as if he rarely got to use the proper side of his desk. Life was tough when you were dealing with superiors.

I took a photo, then went around to the other side of the table. Something crunched under my feet, and then I had to step around Will. Once I was safely on the stranger's side of the table, I took a picture of Craft.

Hmm, that wasn't what I expected.

His face was set into poker mode, but his eyes gave him away. Surprise laced with horror. What had that man said to him? And who was it? He was obviously someone Craft was beholden to. What agent could have that kind of power over another agent? Hopefully Angelica could shed some light on it later. I asked the same question again, but nothing came up. My forehead tightened. What was my magic trying to tell us? I'd never really considered it before, but did my power or the magic river or whatever force organised all this, not show me stuff that was irrelevant? Maybe he met with someone else he didn't want Angelica to know about, but my magic only showed me this particular meeting because it was the only thing that was relevant right now? I would never know unless I tested my theory, and now wasn't the time, but I'd have to remember for later. Or what if another force stopped my magic from showing me everything? I let the horror of that wash through me. I didn't need something else to worry about. Dealing with evil people on Earth was bad enough without thinking there was evil in the magic realm where the river was.

I'd file that away and ask Angelica another day… way in the future.

Angelica stood and held up a brochure. "This looks interesting."

"I've got some interesting stuff too. I think I'm done." I handed her the phone.

Angelica scrolled through the pictures one by one. When she got to the emo guy, her forehead wrinkled. She studied the picture and enlarged it. It was only a slight widening of her eyes, but in a normal person, it was the equivalent of being bug-eyed.

"Who is it?" She totally knew who it was.

Angelica looked at me before staring at Will and Mum. "You'll all want to hear this." Will and Mum both stopped what they were doing and straightened. Angelica handed Will the phone. "Tell me who you see."

Mum blinked, but nothing registered in her face. Will, on the other hand, raised a brow. "What the hell?"

Gah, why were they leaving me in suspense? "Tell me who it is. He looks familiar, but I can't place him." It might have been an agent I'd passed in the hall one day.

Angelica took the phone from Will and angled the screen towards me. "He's in disguise. It's Brosnan."

My mouth fell open. "Oh my God. A visit from Chad and a visit from him. Do you think he was instructed to spy on you, or all of us?" Not that I'd seen Agent Craft before yesterday. Maybe that was because he was trying not to be seen. Hmm….

Her eyes narrowed. "It's likely. But that's not what worries me—we've been careful to protect all our conversations." She looked at Will. "Have you noticed anything unusual when you've been at crime scenes with Lily?"

He shook his head. "No."

"I haven't either. If they knew about my talents, Chad wouldn't have had to cast that spell. I'm betting that they've tried but failed."

She rubbed her cheek. "Maybe. Let's finish going through this." She scanned the wreckage disdainfully. "Then we can go to Chad's office, then home and look more closely at all your pictures. The information we need might be in those documents you've photographed."

I helped rifle through everything and found a brochure for new McLaren cars. "He has expensive taste." I knew what Will earned, and while it was probably in the top 10 per cent of workers, he couldn't afford a one million pounds or more car. "Has he recently inherited, or is this just wishful thinking?"

Will grabbed the knot in his tie and adjusted it. "Why don't you check and see."

I called up my magic. "Show me evidence of Agent Craft ordering or buying a McLaren car." He sat in front of his laptop, a huge grin on his face. I snapped a picture of him, then of the screen, which was a confirmation email from McLaren dated a week ago. *Click.* My eyes bugged at the price. I brought up the picture and enlarged it. "Just over one million pounds. Holy moly." I showed Will, Angelica, and Mum.

Will whistled. "I'm not complaining about what I earn, but you'd be saving up for a while on our wage to buy one of those, especially after you pay tax on your earnings."

Angelica looked at Will. "And you're more senior than him—you earn more." She turned to my mother. "Can you please run checks on his financials? See if any large payments have gone into his account in the last few months. See if he's inherited money or invested in anything that's gone up astronomically lately. If he's earning money on the side from the directors for doing their dirty work, we'll soon find out."

"Surely they wouldn't transfer money to him that can be traced back to them?" Mum asked.

"No, of course not, but the lack of information on the transferor will be a clue in itself."

"I'll get started on that now, then." Mum handed a couple of pieces of paper—hopefully more evidence we could use to piece this thing together—to Angelica and left.

Angelica's phone dinged. She looked at the message. "It's go time. Chad's assistant agreed to an early lunch, and this has taken longer than expected." Will cast an eye around the floor. There was so much crap that the floor was mostly hidden. Angelica raised a brow. "I dare you to say something."

He held up his hands in surrender. "You won't hear a word from me." He did smirk though, which earned him a Ma'am glare. "Ahem, why don't we get to Chadiot's office while we still can."

Angelica raised an eyebrow, then turned and made her way out of the office. I was close behind her. "Are you just going to leave the mess?"

"Yes, dear." If I was waiting for an explanation, I'd best settle in for the long haul. She wasn't one for disclosing her reasoning.

Will locked the office and followed us to the lifts. Before long, we were striding down the long hallway to Chadiot's office. Memories of being taken there by the vampire witch —before I'd known what he was—came back to me. Another witch I'd killed, but he'd left me no choice. As I turned that reality around in my brain, no guilt jumped out to tackle me. Was I turning into a psychopath, someone with no empathy? I bit my lip. Surely not. Was it okay to be unremorseful for killing when it was you or them? I decided that yes, it was. If you don't want me to kill you, don't put me in that situation.

Will's magic tingled my scalp. I looked at him. "Just disabling the cameras in this wing. We have our guy in security today, and he'll wipe any footage of us coming this way; however, we don't know who else has managed to hack into the feed. We can't be too careful."

Angelica nodded. "Agreed." When we reached the door, she stopped, and her magic tickled my scalp. A key card appeared in her hand. A faint blue glow surrounded the key card. "What's that?" I asked.

Angelica made a bubble of silence. "It's my key card to access my office when I was running this organisation. Chad, in his infinite wisdom, didn't change the magical code when he moved in. He either didn't have the talent to re-magic it himself or was too lazy. The fact that he trusted me not to break in also shows the level of arrogance he operates under. I've had a look around, and there wasn't anything new to find in terms of what we've already discovered. It's time to unleash the Lily." She grinned and waved her glowing card in a series of patterns in front of the door. How unlike her to say something intentionally amusing.

I laughed. "Ha, I like it! 'Unleash the Lily.'"

Will chuckled. "I don't want this to go to your head though. It is a good way of saying what we want without anyone knowing. I think it could catch on."

A *click* sounded. Angelica stopped moving the card around and smirked. "Never let it be said that I don't have a sense of humour." She opened the door. "Let's get to it."

Will stopped just inside the doorway. His magic tingled my scalp. He gave a nod. "All cameras in here and his office are disabled for fifteen minutes. I've set it to show an empty office."

"Good work." Angelica started up the staircase to the office. We followed. At the top, the chair at the receptionist's desk was empty—phew—but a guard stood at the door. My eyes widened. Crap!

Angelica made another bubble of silence.

The agent stood straight and gave Angelica a nod. "Hello, Ma'am."

"Hello, Agent Fairchild. How have you been?"

"Good thank you."

"We're just passing through, and you haven't seen us."

His smile was discrete. "Of course."

He unlocked the door and opened it for us, and when we were inside, he shut it. The snap of a lock engaging reached us. What if he wouldn't let us out? Could we travel from here, or were there spells preventing that?

Angelica must've noticed the look on my face. "Don't worry, dear. We can travel out of here. I have this." She held up the glowing card again. "I could've used it to get in, too, but Agent Fairchild was there and has his own code, which requires less effort on my part. And he's one of mine, so don't worry."

"Ah, okay. Great." At this point, I should just assume Angelica had everything covered, but if I didn't ask, how would I learn how it all worked?

"Get started, dear. We don't want to tarry."

This one was tricky. How to word my request that made sense. It was all in the intent though. So maybe I should just say it as best I could and see what happened. "Show me Chad meeting with Craft and proof of what he was asking him to do."

The lighting in his enormous office stayed the same, but Chad was suddenly in his chair, a document open on the desk in front of him. His lips were pressed together in an irritated line, and his bushy eyebrows were drawn down, almost meeting at the top of his nose. One clenched fist rested on the table next to the document. Hmm, interesting. I clicked off a shot, then walked to his side of the desk and focussed on the reason for his anger—a letter from the directors. I pointed my phone at it and clicked off a shot.

I drew more magic. "Where is that letter now?" The same scene appeared on my screen—it was as if the rhymes were chasing me today. Had someone spelled me? Yeah, not likely. I shook my head. *Stop getting distracted.* The squirrel in me was strong today.

Chad sat in his chair looking down, his mouth in an *O* as he stared at nothing. I took a photo. I was just about to ask a different question when someone knocked once on the door. My heart jumped, and I stared at the door.

Angelica kept her voice low. "Out of here. Now."

We made our doorways and skedaddled. I went to James's because I didn't want a disaster in Angelica's reception room. I waited a minute, then made a new doorway home. Angelica was unlocking the reception-room door when I arrived. Will looked at me. "What happened to you?"

"I went via my brother's. I didn't want to chop anyone in half with my doorway." There were still limits to what we could do. Travelling in crowds could still be dangerous.

"Good thinking, dear." Angelica opened the door. Will and I followed her through to the living room. She slid her phone out of her pocket and made a couple of calls as Will and I settled on one Chesterfield, and she settled on the other. Within ten minutes, James, Imani, and Beren arrived. Once everyone was seated, Angelica started the meeting. "We'll begin by looking at Lily's photos on the big screen." Her magic prickled my scalp, and a floating white screen appeared in the middle of the room. She held out her hand, and I stood, leaned over the table, and gave her my phone. She cast another spell, and the first photo appeared.

James chuckled. "That's a nice selfie with the squirrels, Lily. Glad to see you've been spending your time wisely."

I shrugged. "You're just jealous the squirrels have chosen me as their esteemed leader. It's quite a cute picture, actually." In it, I smiled at the phone camera, a squirrel on each shoulder. They were both touching a nose to my cheeks, as if they were giving me a kiss. I'd bribed them with fruit. They were rather cooperative when food was involved. "I should make it my Instagram profile pic. Ooh, maybe I should start a separate account for all the squirrel stuff. Hmm, what should I call it?"

Angelica's brows drew down. "If you've finished, dear, we have urgent work to do."

I frowned and glared at James. "You shouldn't have pulled up that photo. Besides, he started it. You know I have trouble staying on track sometimes."

Will patted my thigh. "Just nobody mention squirrels if you want Lily to concentrate." Beren laughed.

"Pfft. Enough." Angelica waved her hand, and a new image appeared—thankfully, the first photo I'd taken in Craft's office. It was large and easy to read.

Agreement between the PIB Board of Directors Brosnan and Dalton and Agent Paul Craft. Agent Paul Craft agrees to sabotage the PIB within six months from the date of this agreement. The above-named Directors agree to pay Agent Craft the sum of one million pounds on commencement of this agreement. At the end of the six-month period, providing Agent Craft fulfils his obligations under this agreement, a bonus amount of two million pounds will be paid immediately. This agreement is sealed by magic when signed by both parties. Whosoever breaks this agreement shall be subject to death by suffocation at the time of such infringement.

"Holy crap. That's serious stuff." I couldn't believe two of the directors had agreed to die. They must have had access to a colossal amount of money if they were willing to part with that much.

"Yes, dear. I would imagine there's fine print your magic hasn't shown us. I'm surprised the directors agreed to that."

James scratched his ear. "It might be that the pressure on them is coming from somewhere else. Who's powerful enough to threaten them?"

Beren said, "If they're that powerful, they're going to be all but invisible. I don't like our chances of discovering who they are." He looked at me. "Unless we use Lily's talent."

Will shook his head. "Let's not worry about that right now. If we tried to get her anywhere near them, we'd be putting her in grave danger. We're not ready for that step until we've exhausted all other avenues."

"I agree with Agent Blakesley." Thank God Angelica agreed. I didn't feel like putting myself in harm's way again if I didn't have to. Whoever wanted the PIB gone was likely even scarier than Piranha and her father. Gah, not another rhyme. Even I could only laugh at so many rhymes in one day.

Imani must have decided to change the subject to a degree. "What else is on there?"

Angelica looked at the floating screen and brought up the next picture. "The signature page. Everyone's signed. And look at that date—a month ago." Angelica's gaze strayed beyond the screen, and she stared at nothing. After a minute, she looked at me across the coffee table, her poker face discarded for something more vulnerable. I got the distinct impression I was about to be manipulated, which really irritated me. If someone wanted something, they just needed to ask. I knew how important this was.

I cut her off before she spoke. "If you're going to ask me to do something dangerous for the good of the PIB, I accept. I don't need you discarding your poker face to make you seem more… I don't know… needy, like a newborn kitten."

Angelica's head jerked backwards, her chin moving closer to her neck, giving her a double chin. "What?" Her insulted tone almost had me.

I shook my head. "If you need something, just ask. Please don't try and manipulate me into it. Whether you look sad and regretful or not, I'll still make the same decision based on what I believe is right. So, what is it?" Imani's mouth fell open, and Will and Beren looked impressed. James was more startled than anything. Yes, I wasn't usually this blunt with Angelica, but it had been a long day… week, in fact, and I wasn't in the mood.

Her poker face returned—that was something I could deal with. "Okay, dear. If you insist."

"I do."

"If Agent Craft has been recruited, you can bet your favourite squirrel that other agents have been. We need to weed them all out. You're going to have to take photos in every agent's office at headquarters."

Oh, God. What a huge undertaking. The throb of a headache began in my temples. "How many agents are there?"

"One hundred and seventy-four at last count. We used to number over two hundred and fifty, but the last three years have been hell. I suppose we can assume the culling began way before I had any idea what was happening." A glimmer of disappointment passed through her eyes. I would bet that she was upset with herself for not realising it sooner than a few months ago. Nobody was perfect. I would've reminded her, but now wasn't the time, and I didn't think she'd appreciate it. She wasn't much into sharing.

I took a deep breath, ignoring the energy being sucked out of me—just thinking about the work involved was draining. "Of course I'll do it. I take it you want to start tonight when there aren't many agents around?"

Her assessing gaze held approval. "Yes please, dear. I have the roster. We'll obviously start with the agents who are having their day off and aren't expected to return until tomorrow morning. This process might take a week or two, but we need to be thorough, and we can't get caught." She shared a look with James that sent a shiver through me. Did getting caught mean we'd have to eliminate the agent if they weren't on our side? We couldn't exactly let them get back to the directors with the information that we were snooping. They'd know for sure we were onto them. Maybe we'd just kidnap them like we'd done with Chadiot? Gah, this was spiralling out of control quicker than a skydiver with a tangled parachute.

Angelica held up the brochure for the McLaren cars and another brochure for a luxury around-the-world cruise we'd found in Craft's office. "His arrangement with the directors would explain these. We pay well, but not that well." She looked at my phone and brought up the next picture. "Here's one of our esteemed directors in disguise, meeting with Craft."

Imani's brows rose. "Is that before or after they signed the agreement?"

Angelica shrugged and looked at me.

"I'm pretty sure it's after. I asked my magic to show me the last meeting Craft had that he wanted to keep secret from Ma'am. This is what came up."

Angelica looked thoughtful. "Interesting. Something to ponder. It looks as if he agreed to sabotage the PIB, but then they've asked even more than he expected, and he can't get out of it. We can hope it's not something like to kill one of us, but since we can't confirm what it is right now, we'll move on to the photos Lily took in Chad's office." The first photo that appeared on the screen was the one of Chad looking very unhappy. I couldn't help smiling at his upsetness.

"Did someone take his dummy away?" Imani chuckled. I laughed and high-fived her.

The next photo popped up. "Whatever that piece of paper was, it's gone. Is that the point?" Beren asked.

Angelica turned her gaze to him. "Yes. And Lily didn't get a chance to take a photo of the document before we were interrupted. We'll have to go back and see." Her magic tingled my scalp, and a sheet of paper appeared in her hand. Her forehead wrinkled. "Hmm, Agent Piper is on guard duty at Chad's office tonight. He's someone I'm not sure about. I don't want to risk it. We'll just have to wait to find out what was in that document."

James's phone rang. "Hey, Mill." As Millicent spoke on the other end, James's mouth opened slightly, and his eyes widened, then closed. "Dammit." He opened his eyes and blew out a big breath. "Yes, okay. Yep. On it. Thanks. Bye." He shook his head and addressed Angelica. "Agent Craft has just turned up in the PIB reception room."

Imani sat forward. "That's great. Did he have our suspect with him?"

Angelica's gaze stayed with James as she spoke. "I doubt it. What happened, Agent Bianchi? Please tell us the rest of the story." Angelica wasn't the deserving head of the PIB for nothing. She could read her agents like nobody's business, even if they wore a poker face—not that James's face was pokerish.

"He didn't have our suspect with him. Craft's dead."

We all froze, stunned. What the hell? Beren was the first to regain composure. "Did Millicent say how he died? Did he die in the reception room, or did someone transport his body there?"

"They haven't ascertained any of that yet. We'll get over there now, and you can have a look at the body while Ma'am and I check out the scene. Millicent's getting hold of the security tape as we speak."

I rubbed my forehead. This wasn't good. "Do you think that guy managed to kill Agent Craft? Are we protecting his ex-girlfriend? We should at least be restricting her movements anywhere the public is. We don't want a repeat of the train incident."

"No, we don't," Will agreed.

Angelica magicked away the screen. "I have someone on that. We don't have to worry about a repeat of yesterday right now." She stood. "I'm more concerned about how Agent Craft died and why." She looked at Will. "If you could accompany us to the reception room, that would be great." She turned her gaze onto Imani. "I'd like you and Lily to give our idiot friend a visit. See if you can find out what was in that document that had him so upset. Maybe we can use it as leverage, get him to cooperate with us against the directors. There's only a slim chance, but I'll take whatever we can get."

Imani stood. "What if he won't talk?"

Angelica lifted her chin, her stare grave. "You have my permission to use whatever means necessary." Imani opened her mouth to say something else, but Angelica cut her off.

"You heard me. Now go, and be careful. Here are the coordinates."

"Yes, Ma'am."

The coordinates popped into my head. I stood and went to the middle of the room, where Imani and I made our doorways and stepped through. Looked as if Angelica was giving up her secret place to more and more of us. Soon it wouldn't be so secret. As long as the information wasn't tortured out of any of us, it should be good. *Touch wood.*

I put up my return to sender since Angelica had asked us to be careful. If something freaky happened and Chad managed to access his magic and attacked us, I wasn't going to get in trouble for being sloppy.

I halted just inside the living-room doorway, Imani behind me. "Oh, he's had an upgrade." The cage was three times larger than before and took up half the room. Whatever furniture had been down the other end of the room had disappeared. He had a single bed, armchair with footstool, table, bar fridge, a toilet in the corner, and room to walk around. It was almost like the cells at headquarters but a lot less stinky and definitely more luxurious.

Imani looked over my shoulder. "It must be because he's here long term. Ma'am's not totally mean."

"I bet if he had one of us in a cage, it would be as small as he could make it." Anger sizzled along my skin because he didn't deserve any concessions. He would kill or torture us the first chance he got, and up until now, we'd been pretty civil… well, other than locking him up and me feeding him squirrel poo…. Okay, so I wasn't as nice as I thought. At least I hadn't chopped his finger off or something.

Imani nudged my back. "Come on. Let's get this over with. And don't do anything without asking me first."

"I wouldn't dream of it. You're the agent. I'm just the tagalong." That was the moment Chad woke from his nap on his armchair with footstool. He blinked the sleep from his eyes and tried to focus on us.

One corner of Imani's mouth quirked up, and she spoke quietly. "You're way more than that, Lily, but if we can follow protocol as much as possible, I'd feel better. I don't want to have to resort to anything I wouldn't normally."

I moved towards the cage slowly enough that Imani could catch up and take the lead. Chad scrambled out of his chair as we approached. "Let me out of here. This is against the law!"

Imani exaggerated her swagger and smiled. "We're looking out for the best interests of the PIB, which is not against the law. The bureau has done whatever it had to over the years to make sure justice is served, and no one has ever gotten into trouble for it. This is one such time."

"The directors will find me soon, and when they do, you'd better watch out." He waved an angry finger at us. Probably the most exercise he'd done for a while.

I shook my head. "How did someone so pathetic manage to head up the PIB?"

His mouth dropped open. "H— H— How dare you!"

"Oh, sorry. Did I say that out loud? I didn't mean to."

Imani snorted.

I bit my lip. "I didn't mean to, really."

"But do you regret it?" Imani asked.

"Hmm, no. No, I don't." I smiled.

Chad had rushed to the bars closest to us. "But you will regret it. You'll regret everything you've done to me!"

"Meh, promises, promises." Imani was being super cheeky. Was it part of her ploy to rattle Chad and get him to accidentally tell us something? I could definitely help with riling him up so that he exploded with whatever information we wanted. He loved to show off or have one over on Angelica and her team. Maybe this wouldn't be so hard after all?

I knew Imani wanted to take the lead, but I couldn't keep my mouth shut… and did anyone expect anything else? We were within two feet of the cage, and Chad was about a foot from the bars. If he touched them, he'd be electrocuted—not enough to die, but it would hurt. I was surprised he was game to stand that close. "Chad, why do you want to help destroy the PIB?" I couldn't be too specific with my questions because having to come up with an explanation as to why we knew certain things without revealing my secret was asking for trouble.

He folded his arms. "None of your business."

Imani's magic tickled my scalp. What was she d— A Cornetto ice cream appeared in her hand. She took the wrapping off—ooh, chocolate—and licked it. "Mmm, this is yummy."

"Where's mine?" I pouted.

"Here." One appeared in her other hand, and she passed it to me.

"Yum, thanks!" I unwrapped mine and bit into it—I had no self-control. "Mmm." It was so good. I was helpless to resist chocolate in any form… unless it was chocolate sauce spread on Chad. I gagged. *Oh, God, why are you ruining your ice cream, Lily? Idiot. Squirrels. Think of squirrels.* That was better.

Chad watched us. Actually, he was staring at Imani's ice cream, or was that her tongue? Nope, it was the ice cream. She must've known he liked ice cream, or why do this? Whatever, I didn't care—I was getting free chocolate ice cream out of it. Or was she just trying to keep me quiet? I gave her the side-eye, but she didn't react. Okay, so I was being paranoid.

Imani finished her Cornetto and licked her lips. "That was so good." Chad's shoulders sagged. He was a kid who missed out on the treats. Bad luck. How this fit into Imani's plan, I had no idea. I supposed I should just keep watching. "Do you like ice cream, Chad?"

He looked at her warily. "Yes. But you're not going to give me one, are you?"

She smiled. "No. You're uncooperative and a traitor to the PIB. You definitely don't deserve any sweets."

I finished my Cornetto. "That was so good. Thanks, Agent Jawara." I looked at Chad. "I'm not a traitor." I gave him my most smug grin. His narrowed eyes showed I'd hit the mark. Good. I looked at Imani. "His favourite flavour is octopus ice cream." I pretend-stuck my fingers down my throat to indicate gag-inducing.

Imani's eyes widened. "Oh, gross. But then again, it doesn't surprise me. Chad is a gross sort of person." She looked at Chad and cocked her head to the side as if she were sizing him up. "Did you have anything to do with Agent Craft stealing our suspect?"

Chad, being the crappy agent he was, let the surprise ping in his gaze before he turned and hurried back to his armchair. He fell into it and threw his legs on the footstool, pretending to not be flustered. His red cheeks spoiled the effect. "Of course not. I don't even know what suspect you're talking about."

"Oh, that's right." Imani waved her arm dismissively. "You're nobody now. *Of course* you wouldn't know. And as if Agent Craft would do something like that just because you told him to."

I nodded. "Chad's the laughing stock of the PIB. Even I won't do what he says, and I'm not even an agent." I looked at him. "Isn't that right, Chadiot?"

His eyes widened, and he jumped to his feet. "What did you call me?"

"Chadiot. It's Chad plus idiot. Chadiot. Everyone at HQ is using it."

His lips pressed together, and his eyes bugged. Sweat popped out on his forehead. "They are not! You're lying."

I smiled and shrugged. "Okay. If you say so." He he, people hated when you called their bluff, especially man-babies called Chad. I looked at Imani. "I guess he's not really the directors' favourite. I wonder if Ma'am will get a raise at that meeting this afternoon."

Chad hurried to the bars but didn't touch them. "What are you talking about? What meeting?"

Imani shrugged. "We don't know. Ma'am would never tell us her private business, but I do know that she's been looking at Bentleys. She told me she was going to order one next week."

Chad's nostrils flared.

I looked at Imani. "Do you think she'll let me drive it?"

Imani looked at me as if I were stupid. "How would I know? You live there, for goodness' sake."

I smooshed my lips to one side. "Hmm, probably not, then. They're really expensive cars, aren't they?"

"Yes, Lily. Very expensive." She jerked her head around to pin Chad with her gaze. "Did you know..." Imani giggled. She never giggled. This was the performance of a lifetime. "Of course you don't know." She rolled her eyes. "Silly me! Well, I guess I should tell you that Agent Craft actually came back to headquarters. He's agreed to tell us everything about why he took our suspect, and apparently there's some kind of agreement he had with you, or the directors, or something."

Chad's face paled. He was already rather white, but as the

last of the colour drained from him, it was like looking at a blank piece of paper. "That's a lie!"

"Interesting." Imani inspected her nails. She looked up at me and smiled. "Lucky your brother's talent is truth telling. He'll get to the bottom of it soon enough."

"He will. He got the better talent. Honestly, knowing if people washed their hands after they went to the toilet is just a burden." I raised my brow, slid my gaze to Chad, then back to Imani, as if to say, "he doesn't wash his hands." A little colour returned to his cheeks. I smirked.

Imani's magic tingled my scalp, and my phone rang. Chad wouldn't have felt her magic because he was trapped in his cage and had his bracelet on. I slid my phone from my pocket and answered the fake call. "Hello, Ma'am." My mouth dropped open. I grinned and sucked in a breath. "Oh my God! That's awesome! How much?!"

Imani waved her hand in my face and mouthed, "What is it."

"Can you hold on just a moment? Imani's here, and she wants to know." I looked at Imani. "Angelica signed some agreement with the directors. They're paying her five million pounds."

Imani's mouth fell open. "Oh, my word, that's crazy. That can't be right."

I pretended to talk to her. "Imani doesn't believe it. Do you have to do more work, like extra shifts or anything?" Chad was hanging onto every word with both hands, arms, and legs, like a possum clinging to its mother's back. I "listened" to phantom Angelica and nodded, making ooh and ahhh noises. This was too much fun. Who needed TV when you had a Chadiot? "You want to speak to Agent Jawara? Okay. Bye and congrats!" I grinned and handed Imani the phone. "She wants to tell you something top secret."

I quickly magicked a message onto my phone. Imani read it before she put the phone to her ear. "Hello, Ma'am. Yes, we're here with Chadiot. Aha, yes." She made an *O* with her mouth. "Um, are you sure…? Yes. Did they really?" She listened for a while, sucked in a breath, and said, "Okay, yes, Ma'am. You're the boss. Of course. I'll call you as soon as it's done. Bye." She hung up and handed my phone back. She looked at Chad and licked her lips, regret on her face. "As much as I enjoy teasing you, I'm really sorry."

Deep furrows appeared on his forehead. "What, because the directors have put her in charge again? That won't last. And five million pounds? She's not worth more than me." His lips pressed together, and he glared at Imani.

"Oh, no, I'm not worried about you not being in charge. She said the directors have ordered her to kill you. But since she loves delegating, she's given the job to me." Imani smiled as if she'd just told him his ironing would be ready in five minutes. She leaned towards him and whispered conspiratorially, "She actually said you're not important enough for her to kill. She thinks you're too pathetic to waste her time on. I can see her point, can't you?"

He raised his balled fists into the air near his head and waved them around. Scarlett had replaced all the white from his neck up and into his hairline. His ears were practically glowing. "That hoity-toity English witch. How dare she? Damned British snobs. I'll show her!"

I cleared my throat. "From what she said, the directors told her to do it." I looked at Imani. "Didn't they, Agent Jawara?"

"Yes, but they're untouchable." She looked regretfully at Chad. "If only you'd come to her before, when she was trying to find out what was happening with the directors and the PIB. But now they're paying her all that money, I doubt she'd turn on them." She gave him a pouty sad face. "Bad luck." Her expression shifted in an instant, a smile bursting from her face. "Now, how do you want to do this? She didn't tell me I had to make it hurt, so I guess I could do it quickly for you… unless you enjoy pain? There are weirdos who like it. Are you one of them? I mean, you do love octopus ice cream, so anything's possible really."

He swayed, and his head lolled back and around. Was this too cruel? It was definitely a form of torture. Imani could've spelled him to tell the truth and spill everything, but she didn't want to cross that line if she didn't have to. I had to say, this was far worse for the recipient, surely. This wasn't fun anymore. I hated Chad, but I hated being cruel more. As much as I wanted to cave and stop the whole thing, we had to get that information. Lives depended on it—not just the attacker's ex-girlfriend's life, but any potential future victims of other killers… killers that would never be caught if the PIB ceased to exist.

I stared at Imani. "Can you at least make it not messy? And not noisy would be good too. I hate squishy sounds."

She planted her hands on her hips. "Do you want to do it, then? You're being a back-seat killer right now, Lily, and I hate that."

I put my hands up. "No, no, that's fine. You do what you like, but if it's going to get messy, I'll just wait in the kitchen. I wouldn't mind a cup of coffee, actually. Would you like one?" Chad sucked in a breath. He was buying the whole thing, which really was a testament to how little he knew his staff or cared about them. If he'd known us properly, he would've realised we could never do something like this. I eyed Imani.

Or at least he would've known *I* couldn't do something like this. Imani was a trained agent after all. I stopped that line of thinking because she was one of my best friends, and that's how I wanted to see her.

"Not right now, thanks. I've got work to do." Her magic tingled my scalp, and a chainsaw appeared in her hands.

"Oh God, that's messy, and noisy." I turned a curious gaze onto Chad. He swallowed, and his hands shook. "At least I won't have to hear you screaming. That chainsaw will cover all the noise." Chad stumbled back to his chair and fell into it, his body almost as limp as if he were already dead. I turned back to Imani and pointed to the chainsaw. "Have you got any earmuffs where that came from?"

"Good idea." A pair appeared on my head and covered my ears. I smiled and gave her a thumbs up, but worry skittered down my spine. When was he going to cave? How far was Imani willing to take this? Although I shouldn't be too worried, considering we could just compel him to tell us the truth. It might've been a step Imani didn't want to take, but it was better than terrifying him into submission.

I looked at Chad and gave him a wave. "I'd say it was nice knowing you, but it wasn't. You're a mean person, you have a weak moral code, and you're greedy and stupid. You're lucky this isn't going to be a long, drawn-out process. Have fun in the next life." I turned and made my way to the kitchen. God, what if she chopped something off him, like a hand or foot. Being a witch, she could seal the wounds and stop the blood flow, but still... I didn't think even Beren could reattach an appendage, could he?

Muffled voices reached me when I got to the kitchen door. Oh, the earmuffs. I turned around and took them off. Imani stood at the open cage door, chainsaw held up, ready to go, although it was still off. Chad knelt on the floor in front of her, his hands in prayer position. He was crying and babbling. "I'll tell you whatever you want to know. The directors are going to kill you all, you know. We could band together against Angelica and go to the directors, tell them what happened. They would probably pay you lots of money, too, if you helped me and them. You have to believe me."

"You have to answer my questions, or the head comes off." He stared at her like a loyal puppy; her hard gaze had him in thrall, and it even scared me. Cocky Chad had finally disappeared. It was about time.

"I'll tell you anything you want, and you can even put a truth spell on me."

Imani gave me a look that said she'd been waiting for that declaration. She placed the chainsaw on the floor. "Are you sure?"

His frantic nod had me almost feeling sorry for him… but not quite. "Yes, yes, a thousand times yes."

She narrowed her eyes and stared at him as if she didn't believe him and was still considering the deal. God bless her, but she was carrying this act out to the bitter end. I made a mental note to be a bit kinder to him from now on since I'd played a part in his torture. Guilt was an annoying part of my life. Sigh. Why couldn't I be more like Imani and Will and shrug it off? Another reason I could never be an agent.

Imani finally came to her decision. "Okay, but you only get one chance. If you try and resist the spell, all deals are off, and so is your head." My mouth dropped open, and I held off the inappropriate urge to laugh. I knew she was joking… wasn't she?

Chad didn't know she was (probably) joking. He clapped his hands on the top of his head, his dilated pupils swallowing almost all his irises. "Yes, okay. I promise I'll comply. You can put the truth spell on me. I'll answer all your questions. All of them."

Imani gave a nod—decision made. Rather than disappear the chainsaw, she placed it on the ground—a reminder to Chadiot. She looked at me. "Lily, I'll need you for this too. Can you place a no-travel spell on him, please?"

"Of course." I went back over to them. "Chad, can you get out of there, please?" I would've called him Chadiot, but we'd demoralised and angered him enough that he was complying, so there was no point. I didn't want him to change his mind.

He scrambled to his feet and carefully but hurriedly stepped out of the cage before standing in front of us. I drew my magic and said, "Make it so Chad can't travel with magic from here, nor can he walk more than twenty feet in any direction." That should stop him from trying to actually run away too. Power rushed out of me at the initial spell creation, and as we waited for Imani to do her thing, a tiny tug of power constantly drained from the river through me. It was something I could comfortably hold for days if I had to. The slowness of magic drain wasn't heating my blood. I'd eventually fatigue, but it would take a long time.

As Imani created and cast her truth spell, I slid my phone out and pressed voice record. I didn't want to record it on video because Angelica wanted this place to be kept secret, not to mention I didn't want to accidentally film the cage. We weren't exactly in the right from a legal standpoint, even though we were trying to save the PIB. So far, all our proof had been from my talent, and we couldn't submit that to a court. The fine line we trod was thinner than a human hair but hopefully stronger than spider silk.

Imani looked at me. "Grab yourself a chair."

I grabbed one of the padded kitchen chairs and quickly returned. Imani had magicked two armchairs from across the room—she was keeping this close to the cage, which was probably a smart thing to do. Chad wasn't a genius, and I'd spelled him, but snakes could escape from things you didn't expect.

Imani looked at Chad. "Let's start. Please sit." He hurried to comply. Imani and I sat, and I held my power, ready to act in case Chad decided to try something. He had that bracelet on, but, again, you never knew. Underestimating any bad guys, even stupid ones, was a mistake I didn't want to make.

Not wasting any time, Imani pinned Chad with her intimidating agent stare. "Did you ask Agent Craft to do something for the directors?"

"Yes."

"What was it?"

"I asked him, on their behalf, to undermine the PIB and Angelica." Great, now we had the proof without giving away our original source.

"So you and he both had to do that?"

"Yes."

"Would Agent Craft have had to sign an agreement?"

"Yes."

"Did you see that agreement?" I had to hand it to Imani—she was getting to the bottom of things quickly.

"Yes." He sighed. Spilling his guts was killing him—lucky for him that was figurative because Imani easily could've made it literal.

"Was he getting paid the same as you?"

His lips pressed together, and anger flashed in his eyes. "No. He was being paid more. That really got up my nose. He was younger and had less years at the PIB than me. Bloody directors." He folded his arms and sulked. At least the mystery about what he was looking at in the picture I took was probably solved.

"Do you think Agent Craft would have saved a suspect from PIB capture because of his orders to undermine the PIB?"

"Yes." That made more sense than Craft randomly knowing the suspect and wanting to help him. He also likely hadn't been suffering from PTSD—he'd been suffering from PTCD—Pandering Toady Craphead Disorder.

"Which other agents have sworn to the directors or you to sabotage the PIB for money?"

His eyes squeezed shut, and he lowered his head. This was a tough one. Would answering this question kill him as per his orders from the directors? I guessed we were about to find out. He opened his eyes and looked up. "If I answer that question, I'll die of suffocation."

Right. Damn. As much as I hated him, I didn't wish him dead. Plus, we needed more information.

"Okay, don't answer that… yet." Hopefully Imani would come up with a way we could save him and still have him answer. "So, the directors have made you take a death oath?"

"Yes."

"Does every agent they're using have the same agreement as you?"

"No. Mine had more leeway with what I could and couldn't do since I was heading up operations."

"How come you didn't die when I asked about Agent Craft?"

"Because I didn't disclose the name to you. You already knew it. I can't reveal any names you don't already suspect." Hmm, that was an oversight on the directors' parts. That meant he could answer yes/no questions in a court, although they had relied on him not being put under a truth spell. Had they underestimated Angelica? That wouldn't surprise me—a board full of men probably assumed they were superior to a woman. For once, it looked as if the patriarchy had played into our hands.

"Okay, then." Imani pulled her phone out, pressed the screen, and put it to her ear. "Hey, Liv. Can you text me a list of all our agents?" She listened for a moment. "Yes, ASAP. Okay, thanks." She hung up. "If I ask you the names, you can answer me without dying?"

Chad thought about it for a few beats. "Yes." The gods were smiling on us today.

I looked at our prisoner. "Would you kill us if you had the chance?"

His eyebrows jumped up his forehead. "Yes." He scrunched his face in a "doh" moment.

I shook my head. "Double-crossing idiot." I turned my head towards Imani. "At least we know where we stand."

"I always knew, love. A man like this doesn't suddenly honour his promises, unless there's a spell involved." Her phone dinged, and she smiled. "Ah, here we are." Her eyes gleamed as she lifted her gaze and threw the first name at Chad.

The day just got very, very interesting, and we hadn't even killed anyone… yet. I'd call that a win. Now, if only the universe saw fit to throw us a few more.

CHAPTER 9

I mani and I sat at the dining-room table in Angelica's kitchen, a tasty, aromatic selection of Indian food spread in front of us. I looked at my phone. "They were supposed to get here ten minutes ago."

"They're busy, love. Don't worry. They'll be here soon."

The reception-room door opened, and footsteps came down the hallway.

"Speak of the devils." I stood. Angelica walked in first, followed by Mum, James, Beren, Liv, and finally, Will. I greeted him at the door and gave him a kiss. "How was your afternoon?"

He cupped my chin and ran a thumb along my cheekbone. "Productive. I heard yours was even more so." He gave me another kiss. "I missed you today."

"You're so sweet."

James's chair scraped the floor as he pulled himself in. "Can you two lay off the romance? People are trying to eat over here."

I rolled my eyes. "How does Millicent even put up with you, Mr Prude."

"I've told you before: it's only gross when it's your sister."

Will chuckled and planted a mushy kiss on my lips. When he was done, he grinned at James. "The more you complain, the more I'll kiss your sister."

"Argh, I give up. Someone pass me the vindaloo, please."

Will high-fived me and we sat next to each other. Mum smiled and looked at us. "I think you two are sweet. Don't listen to your brother."

James gave her a helpless look. "Now my own mother is turning on me. See what you've done, Lily?"

I shrugged and put a samosa on my plate, then drizzled the yummy green sauce over it. "I can't help it if Mum's normal and you're a nutter."

Angelica finished putting food onto her plate, then looked at Imani. "You've given me a brief rundown of what happened with Chad, but please elaborate."

Imani gave them a recap of our afternoon, including the chainsaw bit. Will and Beren laughed. James looked a tad horrified, as did my mother; Angelica, on the other hand, gave a nod of approval, satisfaction on her face. "I've trained you well, dear. Good."

"Thank you, Ma'am." Her magic tingled my scalp, and a piece of paper appeared in her hand. She gave it to Angelica. "Here's a list of the other eight agents being paid off by the directors."

Angelica held the paper so James could read it as well. They both frowned, their expressions darkening as they finished reading. Angelica looked at Imani. "Thank you for that. This is highly disappointing. Three of those agents were ones I thought I could trust implicitly."

"One of them is someone I've given some choice cases to because I liked him—we get on really well. He and his wife have been to dinner at our house a few times, and vice versa. And that's the thanks we get?" James rubbed his temples. "Where are we going wrong that our own agents are okay with destroying the bureau?"

Mum placed her fork on her plate. "I daresay it's not you who went wrong. The intake system might need tweaking, but don't forget people's circumstances can change. Maybe they're desperate for money, or maybe the job has affected them more than you realised. Seeing the scumbags every day has a profound effect on people. Maybe they're tired of fighting because there's always another bad guy? Or maybe they have other unresolved issues. Don't underestimate the directors' ability to manipulate. They would know these agents' profiles, what they've been through with the PIB and in their lives before us. Make no mistake; they would've preyed on the most vulnerable or greedy, or the ones who want power more than justice."

James noisily blew air out of his nose. "I know. It still sucks."

Mum rubbed his back. "I know it does, honey, but that's life."

My old companion sadness settled a heavy arm over my shoulder. James rarely showed how upset he was—this had obviously rattled him. There were only a few things worse than a friend letting you down, and this wasn't just a no-show at dinner; this was a biggie. I hated seeing my brother hurting. To distract him more than anything, I asked, "Are we going to go after them or just watch and wait?"

Angelica swallowed the food in her mouth. "Watch and

wait. I'll assign them to smaller cases, keep them away from the important stuff."

Will smirked. "You could set up some surveillance for them to do on vacant premises." That got a small smile from James.

Beren laughed. "Nice one. Surveillance is boring at the best of times, let alone when there's nothing to see."

"Yes, dears, I could, and I think we will for a pair of them, but if we're too obvious, they'll soon figure out that we're onto them." Angelica turned to Imani. "Do the agents know about each other?"

"No. Chad said they didn't want them to accidentally give away the others. They also didn't want them teaming up to betray the directors if they changed their minds."

James pushed his food around his plate with his fork. "Two of them are among our top assassins. I'm sure that's not a coincidence on the part of the directors."

My eyes bugged wide. "Assassins?!"

James gave me a "you have to be kidding" look. "Of course. I doubt there's any top government law-enforcement agency that doesn't have them. They do normal agent duties, but if we're called on by any of the other government agencies to add our firepower, we send them. I'll admit, the PIB doesn't tend to assassinate people, but just in case we need to take someone out, they're there."

"Um, right." I eyed everyone around the table. "None of you are assassins, are you?"

"No." James's tone was reassuring, but I still gave him a sceptical look.

Angelica looked at me. "Can we please get on with it?"

"Sorry."

She turned back to James. "Right. Well, it can't be helped, but at least we know who they are." She pulled her gaze away from James and regarded each one of us. "Team, be extra careful around those agents."

She didn't have to tell me twice. "Does that mean Liv and Mum will be vulnerable at headquarters? Should we assign them an agent each?"

"Millicent would be happy to make sure Liv is safe—they work in the same office, so it won't be difficult to organise. I'll have a word to her when I go home tonight."

"Okay, thanks." Beren gave James a nod.

"And I can make sure Kat is with me—or, at a pinch, one of you—all the time." Angelica turned to my mother. "Is that okay? We'll be coming and going a fair bit."

Mum smiled. "Sounds fine to me."

Imani took a swig of water. "What happened with Craft? Did you get any answers as to how he died?"

Beren looked at Imani. "He died by suffocation, and there was a faint magic signature. But it didn't belong to one of the directors. Doesn't show up in our system either."

"One of their secret criminal friends, maybe? It wasn't our suspect, was it?" Imani asked.

"Possibly a criminal friend. As you know, the PIB holds records for any witches in the armed forces, and Larsen's magic signature is different to the one we found." Beren shrugged. "The one good thing was that Craft had his phone on him. Millicent's getting hold of his internet-company's records to see where he was. Once she's goes through which towers his phone pinged, we might be able to find our suspect. She said she'll have an answer for us tonight."

"Who's looking after Annabelle?" My poor niece wasn't seeing much of her parents lately.

"Millicent's working from home tonight," James answered. "I could've given it to someone else, but in light of what's been going on, I don't trust anyone outside of our group. And while we now know about those eight other agents, the directors could recruit new ones at any time."

"Gah, that sucks." Something else bothered me. "Do you think the directors know that Craft's dead?"

Angelica wiped her mouth with her napkin. "I have no idea. If they don't already, they will soon. But they won't know that we're cognisant of his agreement with them. What they will do, though, is worry that we'll look into it. Unfortunately, they've covered all their bases. It's going to be hard to trace any of this back to them without a truth spell on Chad, which is inadmissible in court."

"So many hurdles, but we'll jump them eventually. I have faith in all of us." Mum smiled proudly. "I found the transaction for the first million pounds. It was sent by a shelf company with an account in the Cayman Islands."

James laughed. "So original."

"So effective." Imani frowned.

Mum's smile fell. "Yes, unfortunately. And the director is listed as Donald Duck."

My mouth dropped open. "You're kidding. How the hell do they get away with that?"

Angelica sighed. "No one cares, dear. It's the sad state of our world today."

"But we care." Will grabbed my hand. "Don't worry, Lily. We won't ever give up trying to make the world a better place."

I squeezed his hand. "I know. I just wish it didn't require constant work and risk. It never ends."

"No, it doesn't." Angelica's face was grim. "And it's going to get a whole lot worse before it gets better."

I sighed. "Please don't remind me. What about that

rescheduled meeting Chad is supposed to have with the directors?"

Angelica sighed. "We're into the mud so deep that I think we're past worrying about keeping ourselves clean. I'm going to cast a coercion spell on him, and Lavender can hide it for me. There's no other way if we want to avoid suspicion." She took a deep breath and looked each of us in the eyes in turn. "There's too much at stake. What we do in the next few weeks or months will determine the safety of witches and non-witches alike for years. We can't let them destroy the PIB. We won't." Her straight posture and the determination shining from her eyes had me nodding. As much as I wanted to be the head of a squirrel army, Ma'am was the person to inspire and lead us humans to victory. I didn't envy the job she had ahead, but I trusted her to steer us in the right direction.

"I'm behind you all the way, Ma'am." I smiled. "I'll do whatever it takes."

She stared at me. "Be careful what you promise, Lily. I may have to ask you to do things you consider unconscionable."

I was no longer smiling, but I was just as resolute. "I know. I won't let you down."

"None of us will," said James. Everyone nodded and promised unwavering support. The strong bond we already shared just became unbreakable. Love infused my heart, and tears briefly warmed my eyes. We had all stood together for so long and achieved so many incredible things in dangerous circumstances. If anyone could beat the directors and keep the PIB alive, it was us.

James's phone rang. "Hey, hon. That's excellent. Yes, send it through." He listened for another minute. "Okay, thanks. Love you. Bye."

I opened my mouth and pretended to stick my finger down

my throat and vomit. "Ew, that's gross. You said you loved her." He gave me a "ha ha, very funny" look.

Will grinned. "Nicely done."

I blew on my fingernails and smirked. "Why, thank you."

James rolled his eyes, then turned to Angelica. "Millicent's found the coordinates of where Craft was straight after the train incident, and then for the next few hours after that. We can start there, and she'll give us the other locations for just before he died when we've done that."

"Excellent." Angelica gave a nod.

James's phone dinged with a message. "I'll forward them to you, Ma'am."

Her phone dinged. "Thank you." She opened the message and read the contents. "Hmm, interesting." She looked up at Will. "Looks like you lot are off to Switzerland." I knew this was an investigation, but my face must have lit up too much because she shook her head at me. "No, Lily. You're staying here, as is Agent Bianchi. I'm leaving this one to Agents Blakesley, Jawara, and DuPree." I sighed. There was no point arguing. I'd save annoying Angelica for something more special than ten minutes walking from a public toilet to wherever the property was. Something Dad always used to say was pick your battles. My gaze strayed to the table. If only he were here. I looked at Mum. I kept forgetting she'd lost him too. Stupid RP. Thank God we'd gotten rid of them.

Will shoved a huge chunk of garlic naan into his mouth and stood. Beren smiled. "Looks like it's time to go." He gave Liv a quick kiss and stood. She'd been awfully quiet for the entire meeting. But then again, her opinion hadn't been required. I'd only spoken because I was nosy, and I couldn't keep my mouth shut.

Liv's expression was serious when she said, "Be careful." He gave her a reassuring smile.

Angelica looked at Imani as she stood. "Here are the coordinates, Agent Jawara."

"Thank you."

Angelica looked at Beren and Will, and they gave her a nod. I had to assume that she'd sent the coordinates to them too. "This is for a public toilet in Lucerne. I'll text you the address of the property he was at for the first thirty minutes after snatching our suspect. I don't need to say this, but I will —be on guard. Assume someone is waiting for you. Be prepared."

Will gave her a nod. "Always."

Angelica pressed her phone screen a couple of times, and Will's phone dinged with the message. "You should all be good to go. If you nab the suspect, take him straight to headquarters and call me. I'll meet you there, but I also don't want the word to get out. The less that gets back to the directors, the better. Let them think they have the upper hand."

I didn't say anything because it wasn't productive, but they kind of did have the upper hand so far. We were scrambling to survive. They were sitting around their expensive boardroom table eating caviar and drinking ten-thousand-pound bottles of champagne. Okay, so maybe my imagination was taking over, but, still, you know what I mean.

While they were gone, we ate a quiet dinner. It was stressful not knowing what was happening. Was Matthew alive or dead? Was he even there, or had Craft taken him to Switzerland then somewhere else? When we finished eating, they weren't back. Angelica and I magicked everything clean and away. This was the one time where doing things the non-witch way would've been good—I needed a distraction.

Angelica stood at the doorway. "Why don't we all have a relaxing cup of tea in the living room?"

Sitting down and relaxing was the last thing I was capable of. Liv cocked her head to the side as she regarded me. "What's up, Lily? They'll be okay."

"I know, but I can't stand waiting. I need to do something."

She smiled. "On a scale of one to ten squirrels, how much nervous energy do you have?"

I laughed. "A solid eight-squirrels' worth."

Her eyebrows jumped. "Oh, wow, that's a lot. Maybe go climb a tree. It might make you feel better." Mum laughed, and even one corner of Angelica's lip curled up.

A knock on the reception-room door made us all turn and look down the hallway. "I'll get it." Angelica walked at a normal pace to the door when I wanted her to run. What happened? If Will and everyone were back, it meant they hadn't found Matthew Larson's body. Had they found him alive and decided to bring him here?

I drew my power and moved to the doorway, blocking anyone from coming in here to attack Mum and Liv. Not that Angelica would let anyone get that far, but after everything I'd been through, caution had become my middle name. I stood, feet shoulder-width apart, hands next to my hips like a gunslinger. Hmm, why weren't we called magic-slingers? I quite liked that term. I'd never become an agent, but I could be a magic-slinger. Maybe I should get cards made up—Lily Bianchi, photographer, squirrel lover, and magic-slinger.

"Lily, why are you blocking the doorway?" Angelica stood there staring at me.

"Oh, sorry." I stepped out of the way and let her, Will, Imani, and Beren back in.

James got in first. "So, what happened?"

"Obviously, he wasn't there." Beren pulled out a chair and sat. Will sat next to him. Imani just stood there, arms folded.

"Did you find anything, dear? Do we need Lily to investigate?"

Will shook his head. "There was a small amount of blood on the carpet—not enough to be a serious injury. It could, in fact, be the remnants of when Craft made his doorway. I took samples. Beren's going to put them through the lab tomorrow."

Beren rubbed the back of his neck. "I want to supervise the testing myself, make sure no one knows where it's from and what it is. I'm going to get Dr Finch on it. She's not on our compromised-agents list. She's kept results off the records for me a couple of times before, so it should be okay."

Imani pulled something small out of her pocket and handed it to Angelica. "I found this sitting on the floor under a table. It was in a hotel room—he'd booked it out for a week, about ten minutes after he took Larsen. The woman on hotel reception was a witch. She was very respectful of us. Apparently the Swiss PIB brought her stalker to justice, so she was happy to answer all our questions and give us access to the room. I did tell her he wouldn't be coming back."

"What about paying for it? Was she upset he'd done a runner?" Okay, so he hadn't intentionally not returned, but as far she knew, he had.

Imani looked at me. "No. He'd prepaid... with cash."

"He didn't want us to trace him," James theorised.

"Or," Angelica said, "he didn't want someone else to find him?"

Will raised a brow. "You thinking he wanted out of his contract?"

Angelica made her way to the table and sat. "Possibly. He

ended up dead, didn't he? And it was the death agreed to on the contract. Maybe they asked him to do something he couldn't stomach?"

I slid into the seat next to Angelica. "But how did he end up at headquarters? Did he make a doorway as he suffocated, or did the directors know and send him there as a warning?"

Angelica shook her head. "The directors don't know we know anything… yet. I would say that he made his own doorway. Maybe he wanted to warn us when he realised everything was going to go south? Or maybe he felt remorse for taking our suspect and wanted us to find him?"

"So, let's assume he did take our suspect to that hotel room," Will said. "Did Craft move him from that hotel room, or did someone else?"

Angelica held Imani's find up. "This is a card for a real-estate agent. There's an address scrawled on the back. I'd say we get Lily to that hotel room to look into this further, but let's check this out first. I don't want to expose her any more than I have to."

I frowned. "But I'm happy to help. It's not like there's anyone there but the friendly front-desk lady, and she won't see what I do when I go into the room. It'll clear up whether someone else took Larsen."

Will looked at me. "I agree with Angelica. If this other address is nothing, we'll get you in there, but until then, sit tight."

Mum made her way to Angelica and held out her hand. "Let me see that. I'll check whether there's anything in his bank account to tie him to this agency. Can you just magic me my laptop from your office?"

"Of course." Angelica's magic tingled my scalp, and Mum's computer appeared on the table. She handed Mum the card. Mum sat at the table and turned her computer on. She shuddered. "I've just had a sense of déjà vu."

"Are you okay?" I asked.

She shrugged. "Yes. I have no idea what it was." She smiled. "It was probably nothing. Maybe just me getting back into the swing of working. Sometimes I'll do something similar to what I'd done at work, years ago, and it'll come back to me." She put her hand up as if to say, oh well, then lowered her gaze to her computer screen.

Imani and Liv, the last ones standing, finally decided to join us at the table. Imani folded her arms and rested them on the wooden surface. "How are we going to spin this if we find Larsen isn't alive?"

Angelica smoothed her bun. So, she hadn't thought about this yet, or at least not enough to have come up with a solution. "I haven't decided yet." I held my smile in check. That was Angelica spinning an "I don't know" into something that made her sound more like she knew what she was doing. Typical that she wouldn't show any weakness, even to the people who loved her.

Imani turned to James. "Why don't you check out the coordinates Millicent sent you, and we can cross reference it to this other address, see if he's even been there? Maybe it has nothing to do with anything."

James shrugged. "Okay. We have nothing to lose." He opened his phone and pulled up the message she sent. He scrolled through the information. Before he finished, Mum looked up from her computer.

"I've found it. Here." She turned her laptop around for everyone to see. She'd enlarged the page, and the information was in the middle. The payment was for two thousand eight hundred pounds, and it was marked "rent 1 mnth." I hated how the bank never gave you enough space to write a lengthy description. It was super irritating. Surely with all their technology, they could give us a few extra spaces.

"Is that the first payment?" Angelica asked.

"Yes. It's dated three weeks ago. He was possibly living here?"

James tapped his fingers on the table. "Maybe that's why he didn't go back to his apartment. But why would he take the guy to his house when he could've kept him at the hotel?"

Imani looked at James. "He could've been scared a cleaner or someone would discover him. He might have killed the guy and just buried him somewhere in the forest. His other place could be a total dead end."

Angelica cast a cool gaze over us. "Well, there's only one way to find out. This time, I want Lily there. She's less likely to be seen going to a private home. If there's nothing there, she can take pictures and hopefully shed some light on what, if anything, has happened at his house." She cocked her head to the side. "In fact, I have nothing better to do, so I'll join you all." She looked at Mum. "Before we go, I'll take you both to Millicent's. She could do with some help, and if anything happens and we need to act quickly, there'll be less back and forthing. Less communication means less chance our information will be intercepted. We take every precaution, but for all we know, they have new spying spells we can't detect." Once that was decided, she ferried them to my brother's, then returned via the reception room. "What are the coordinates, Agent Jawara?"

Imani sent them to us. I put them on my doorway and stepped through.

After exiting the toilets, which also incorporated change rooms, we left a two-storey building. "Where are we?" I hated not knowing where we were, and it was dark. Not that knowing would change anything, but I supposed it was always good to know where one's been.

"Exeter," Will said. "This is a sports club. We have a two-mile walk to get where we're going."

As we exited the car park and entered a residential street, Angelica said, "Put up your return to senders and your no-notice spells if you haven't already." I looked at everyone with my other sight. I was the only one who hadn't put up their return to sender. Of course I was. Just when I thought I was getting the hang of everything, I forgot something crucial. I did as Angelica had asked. "This looks good." She nodded at a white Volvo station wagon. Her magic tingled my scalp, and she opened the door.

I frantically looked around, paranoid about being found out. Not that it mattered. Angelica would probably bend the rules and mind wipe anyone who saw us. "Why are we stealing a car?" I couldn't help asking. We could jog two miles. It wasn't that far.

"I'm not walking or running two miles. I'm not in the mood. You're welcome to get in the car, dear, or go home."

I gave her a look, and Will smiled. "Don't worry, Lily. We'll return the car. They won't even realise we borrowed it."

When he put it that way, it didn't sound so bad. "*Fine.*" I opened the door and hopped into the back. Will got into the driver's seat, Angelica into the front passenger seat, and Imani and Beren got into the back on either side of me. Imani hip bumped me. "You're the smallest. You can sit on my lap, otherwise James is going to have to run."

James stood outside waiting. I was going to mention that it

was illegal and unsafe, but I didn't want to be told to go home again, and the longer I stalled, the more chance of someone noticing we were stealing a car, so I hopped on and held the headrest of Will's seat. Beren shifted over into my spot, and James got in.

Will got us to the property in not much time at all. A short gravel driveway led to a two-storey brick farmhouse, probably built in the early 1900s. No lights were on, and Will drove straight up to the single detached garage.

My heart rate kicked up a notch. "What if someone's home? What happened to being stealthy?"

Angelica turned in her seat and looked at me. "There are six of us. I doubt there'll be more than six trained agents in that house. In fact, I would think we'd be lucky to find the man we're looking for. This expedition is also about finding more information. This location is secret and removed enough that Agent Craft might've stored documents here or met with the directors." Ah, so that's why I was really here.

Her explanation opened the door to relief, which spilled through me. My heart rate went back to normal. "Okay."

"Just to be on the safe side, though, dear, you and Imani stay here while the rest of us make sure the house is clear." I rolled my eyes. I didn't need babying… but then again, I was being a chicken. Why was I worrying so much? Was it PTSD? I'd had a few counselling sessions with a trained PIB psychologist since we'd returned from Venice, and I was feeling more like my old self, but it probably took longer to get over things. Typical of my impatient self to expect to get over it in five minutes.

Will, Beren, James, and Angelica got out of the car and left their doors open. In the darkness, I could just make out each of them taking their guns out. Not dangerous, my bottom. Instead of feeling more secure that they were armed, the fact that they wanted to be armed dredged up adrenaline. I opened the portal and readied to reach for the power.

In the gloom of night, Angelica and Will carefully made their way to the front door. James and Beren headed for the back of the house, glancing around and at the first-floor windows as they rounded the corner.

I stared as Will and Angelica neared the front porch. The scent of honeysuckle floated in through the open doors, the sweetness at odds with the apprehension tightening my shoulders. *Don't be silly—there's probably no one there.* Maybe I should just read a book on my phone while we waited.

My phone rang, and I jumped so high I almost hit my head on the car ceiling. Imani snorted. "You nutter."

The need to speak softly was overwhelming. "It's Mum." I answered it, keeping my voice low. I wasn't sure if it was because I wanted to hear what was happening at the house or if I was just scared someone would hear me. "Hi. What's up?"

"Where are you?"

"At the house. We just got here. Imani and I are waiting in the car for the all-clear."

"You have to warn Angelica. I tried to warn her, but she must have her phone off because she's sneaking around. I figured out what the déjà vu was about."

"What?"

"I remembered that house address. It came up in a case I was working, years ago. It belonged to a mob boss back then, and I've just checked that it still does. This is too much of a coincidence. You have to let Angelica know."

"Okay, going right now. I'll call you back."

"Hurry, and be careful!"

I hung up and spoke to Imani as I scooted out of the car. "This could be a set-up. This house belongs to a mob boss."

"Oh, crap." She jumped out the other side and drew her gun, but neither of us approached cautiously—Will and Angelica had gone inside while I'd been on the phone.

We ran. The gravel crunched under our frantic footsteps.

But were we panicking for nothing? What if it was just a huge coincidence?

Yeah, right. Also, better to be safe than sorry. If we were overreacting, we could all laugh about it later.

I took a deep breath before we plunged through the front entryway, then into a living area—if something happened, what was it going to be? Were witches hiding in cupboards? Was there a bomb rigged to go off? That's what would happen in the movies, and, honestly, I felt like I lived in a movie most of the time.

Will shouted from somewhere inside, "I found him! He's dead." The fact that he was calling out probably meant I could too.

"Don't touch anything! Come here. Mum called." Imani looked at me with a "what are you doing?" expression. "What? Will called out. If anyone is hiding here, they know we're all inside. This can't wait. Have you checked if there's any spells on the house?"

"It's not that easy, and no." She stopped walking and frowned. "We should stay here." She threw her head back and yelled. "Ma'am, agents, to me. Now!"

Within seconds, the four of them sprinted through the door, glowing with magic and guns at the ready. Beren kept a lookout at the door they'd just come through while Angelica came straight to us. "What's all this about?"

"I just received a call from Mum. She said this is a mob

boss's home. She finally realised where she'd heard of it. She checked it out, and it's still owned by that family, or guy, or whatever."

Anger flickered through her eyes, and she spun to face Imani and James. "Get a read on the spells on this house." She turned to me. "Nobody leaves until we sort this out." Why was she targeting me with that order? Maybe the fear was plastered across my poker-challenged face.

"Shouldn't we get out of here ASAP?" Call me stupid, but wasn't that the safest course of action? Hmm, that's probably why she'd directed it at me. I was probably the only one here thinking of their safety.

Angelica shook her head. "No. There could be a leave-kill spell." *Oh.*

"Leave-kill?" My eyes widened. That was a harsh name for a spell.

Imani's voice was firm but soothing. "If that spell's involved, when we leave, either by magic or the normal way, we'll die."

"How will we die?"

She shrugged. "There are several ways. The house could be rigged to blow up, or electrocute us, or maybe intense pressure will crush us."

"Oh, great. Death-magic bingo. What's on my card today?"

James frowned. "You didn't have to come. Maybe learn to say no more often."

Anger pulsed up through my body and found an outlet in my glare. "James, don't be so mean. I'm trying to help." I folded my arms and slapped them on my chest.

He shut his eyes briefly. "I'm sorry. I'm just worried. Having you here is a distraction. Imagine if we both died.

What would happen to Mum?" Gah, the guilt trip. To be fair, this wasn't my job, but it was his.

"Enough of this morbid and unproductive talk." Angelica's tone was in full "don't argue with me" mode. "I asked Lily to come because we need her. I'm sorry for putting you in this situation, Agent Bianchi, but if you can't handle your sister helping us, maybe you should assign yourself a different role in future when I've asked her to assist."

He stared at her, many unsaid things flashing through his eyes. "Yes, Ma'am."

Her voice was gentler this time. "Don't question my motives... ever. I know what I'm doing."

"Yes, Ma'am."

Guilt flushed my face. Poor James cared, and he was getting in trouble. Gah, this was why they said never work with friends or family.

"Sorry, James. I didn't know. I'll consider you in future."

Care shone from his eyes. "I'm sorry. I shouldn't have said anything. It's my issue. I'll always worry about you, Lily, but you have to make your own choices based on what you feel, and only that." We exchanged sheepish smiles.

Will put his hands on his hips. "I'm glad you've sorted that out. Let's get back to why we're here." His gaze travelled from James to Imani. "While you two work through this other issue, I'm going to go back and check out the body."

"Don't touch it," Angelica demanded.

"I won't. Actually, Lily, can you come with me? I think you should take some photos. Let's see if Agent Craft set this whole thing up, or if the directors had a hand."

Angelica's mouth pinched into a small, squished line of disgust—probably with the directors being such crapheads rather than Will's suggestion of getting back to work. "Good idea, Agent Blakesley. Stay alert."

"Of course." He gave a nod and gestured at me to follow. When we got to the bedroom containing the body, Will turned to me. "Just a sec. Checking for cameras and bugs." His magic tingled my scalp. After a couple of minutes, he pointed to a corner near the ceiling. *Pop!* Smoke rose from a marble-sized ball of a camera that just materialised. *Pop!* I jerked my head around. The one in the opposite corner appeared and was just as ruined. He dusted his hands together. "Now, we can start."

I held my phone up. "Show me who brought Matthew Larson to this room."

A humungous man, who looked like a bear without fur but wearing a suit, held the captive in his short, beefy arms and was placing him in the chair. It looked as if Larsen was already dead. I snapped a photo. Was Craft already dead when this was taken? Had he really died from going against their wishes, or had they killed him to make it look that way? But why do that when they didn't know we knew? Or did they know? I squeezed my eyes shut and shook my head to stop the useless thoughts.

"Lily, are you all right?"

I opened my eyes. "Yes, sorry. Just trying to stop the slippery slide into my squirrel brain. I have another question to ask my magic."

"Okay."

"Show me if Agent Craft was in this house on the day the dead man was here." Nothing appeared. I turned and left, Will on my heels. Holding my phone up, I traversed the hallway, stopped at each doorway, and leaned in, until I'd made my way back to Angelica, Imani, and Beren. Nothing. "According to my talent, Agent Craft wasn't here at all the day that body was brought here—whether that was today or yesterday, I can't say. I guess I could ask."

"Yes, please, dear. That would be good. Your talent is extremely useful. The fact that you can narrow down time frames is exceptional."

The warm and fuzzies swarmed my heart, bringing a smile to my face. "Thank you." I hurried back to the bedroom to check. "Show me Larsen here yesterday." Nothing. "Show me Larsen here today. The same scene as before showed up. And there we had it. "They brought Larsen here today."

Angelica stood at the bedroom door. "I don't want to make any more assumptions right now about what Craft had decided or not decided until we get a rough time of death for our dead guy."

Beren looked into the room over Angelica's shoulder. "I can take a look, but I'll have to touch him."

She held up her hand for him to wait. "I'll check with Agent Jawara, see if his body is linked to any spells on the house." She turned and left. My phone rang. "Hey, Mum. We're inside. Nothing's happened… yet."

"Oh, thank God. I was worried when I hadn't heard from you."

"Well, there might be a spell prohibiting us from leaving that we'll have to work through."

She gasped. "Not a leave-kill spell?"

"Ah, yeah." How did everyone know about this but me? Oh, that's right; I wasn't an agent. Did they have a list of spells they had to learn about? Maybe I should ask for that list so I'd be better prepared for stuff. And why had they rushed in if that spell could've been in play? I supposed if they checked for every single possible thing before raiding a house, they'd never catch anyone.

"Oh, no, Lily. That's not good."

"Way to make me feel better, Mum. I'm sure we'll figure it out—we do have the top agents in the bureau on it."

"Tell Angelica that if she needs my input, let me know. I've dealt with a couple of those before, but then again, so has she. Still, tell her to call when she knows what's happening. And if she needs anything."

"Okay, Mum. I will."

Worry vibrated through her voice. "Stay safe, sweetie."

"I'm with the best of the best. We'll be fine. Bye, Mum. Love you." Did I believe myself? Yes and no. I was with the best of the best... hell, I was one of them, but we weren't invincible. I'd learned that lesson the hard way. I shuddered at the bittersweet memories of Venice.

"Love you. Tell your brother I love him too. And I'm so proud of you both." Wow, this was starting to sound like a final goodbye. The only thing missing was the sobbing. I'd better get off the phone before that happened.

"I will. Bye."

"Bye."

I stuck my head into the hallway and called out to James. "Hey, bro, your mum sends her love and says she's proud of you."

He came out of the living room and stood in the hallway. "Ah, okay. Why the message? It's not my twenty-first." He chuckled.

"I think she thinks we're done for."

"Lily!" Angelica called out. "Enough of the morbidity, I said."

"Ha, I know, but you forgot to tell my mother."

Beren snickered. "You guys are hilarious. You always make a dangerous situation fun."

Will laughed. "That's a skill, right?"

I smiled. "That's one of the nicest things anyone's ever said to me. Thanks, B."

"You're welcome." He waggled his brows.

Imani came into the hallway. "James, based on what you found, what do you think of this?" Her magic tingled my scalp, and a 3D image appeared in the air. Impressive. Ordering light to do your bidding. Or was it dust motes reflecting light? Who knew? I blew out a breath. Why was there so much to learn? "This is a spell signature I've managed to extract from the tangle."

James stared at the construct floating near his head. "I counted three spells, but I didn't pick what this was out of that mess. Good work."

Imani gave a nod. "Thanks. I haven't seen it before, but it has a similar make-up to a leave-kill I studied during training."

"Sorry to interrupt, but what are the other spells you found?" This was a great discovery, but were the other spells bad?

James looked at me. "I identified an alert spell. Whoever planted this knows someone's here, and I would bet they have cameras planted around the place, so they also know it's us."

"Yeah, I found two in here," Will said from the doorway.

"The other one I identified was a keep-clean spell."

"What?" That seemed like a waste of energy, unless the owner was a germophobe.

Imani tapped her chin. "Probably so they didn't have to clean or expose this place to anyone by getting cleaners in. Especially if you're going to bring dead bodies here...." She looked at James. "The spell I found tangled with the leave-kill was a confirm-or-die spell for anyone coming via the reception room. If the door isn't answered within a minute of someone arriving, the unlucky arrivee has to punch a code in. If they get it wrong three times or take too long to put in the right code, poisonous gas comes in."

Beren's eyes widened. "That's extreme."

Angelica's poker face was as bland as it could get. "They seem like extreme sort of people. I'm betting this was all created by the crooks our directors are in bed with." She looked at Imani. "So, what damage are they inflicting? How do we get out of here alive and with all appendages intact?"

"I haven't gotten that far. Maybe we can all help decipher it." Everyone turned and stared at the floating symbol. I had no idea where to start, so, for once, I kept my mouth shut.

Imani reached up and pushed the bottom corner of it with a finger. It turned slowly until she was looking at the opposite side. "It's so complex. Whoever did this has exceptional talent."

Angelica walked over and stood with her face close to it, peering into its centre. She pointed to a thick mass of squiggles. "This is the bit that gets me." She moved her finger to the outside and traced along a straight line till it curved and looped. "This is the explosion part."

"The *what?* We're going to explode?"

She gave me a deadpan look. "We're not going to explode, dear. We'll get out of this. Don't worry."

"Famous last words," I mumbled. The concerned side-eye James gave me reinforced my point.

Will rested his large, warm hand on my shoulder. "We *will* figure this out. Have faith."

"What have I got to lose?" I stared at him and raised my eyebrows.

He smiled. "At least we'll go together."

My mouth dropped open, and Imani snorted. I flicked my gaze to her. "Don't you start."

She grinned. "Look at it this way, Lily. If we die in an explosion, it'll be quick and relatively painless, and you'll hardly know what happened."

"Gah, how did I get stuck with you lot?" Maybe I should reconsider this whole living-in-England thing and go back to Australia as soon as I got the chance. *If* I got the chance.

Angelica smirked and continued her assessment. "If you'll all look this way, please. Feel free to tell me if I'm wrong." Her expression said that was never going to happen, but she'd be gracious about the fact that possibly it might happen in an alternate universe. "This small triangle here in the middle will activate the spell if we try and dismantle it."

Beren whistled. "Impressive. Whoever made it is losing power to this baby every day."

"Could we just outwait them?" I asked.

"I'm afraid not, dear. They could feed this spell for a few weeks if that's all they did, and we don't have weeks. By then, the PIB will be history. If we're not there to make sure the bureau isn't destroyed, we'll leave this house and return to chaos."

"But if we die, the PIB will anyway." Surely she could see my logic. I'd rather be alive in a chaotic world we could possibly fix than be dead.

"True, dear, but I don't think we will. Our group has more than enough power to survive this if we make sure we think it through properly."

James was still facing Angelica, but he gave me another speedy side-eye. Was he tossing up Angelica's odds and not finding them as favourable as she wanted us to?

"Hang on." Imani stretched her head forward. "This zigzag, that's a travel spell."

Will's eyes widened, and he went around to stand next to her and look. "Jesus, you're right."

Foreboding itched my nape. "What does that mean?" This wasn't going to be good. I shouldn't have asked, but, well, you know me. I couldn't stand not knowing. Imani and Will shared a look, meaning they did not want to tell me. "Just tell me. I'm stuck in this crap now. I deserve to know the facts."

Angelica jerked her chin up in the universal sign for "go on." Everyone else looked at each other until every gaze was pinned on Will.

Looked like he drew the short straw.

"After the explosion, it will send our bodies somewhere— probably so they can confirm we're dead."

I blinked. Oh, for God's sake. "You're saying that if we manage to survive being blown up, we'll have to escape from somewhere else?"

Will shrugged. "You asked. Next time, don't."

I cast an agitated gaze around the circle of my friends. "How can you all be so calm? We're going to die! And even if we don't, we probably will later."

"You could say that about any situation, Lily." Imani's brown-eyed gaze was unwavering. "If we panic, we're guaranteed not to get out of this. You know thinking logically and calmly is the way to go. You're not a panicker. We wouldn't have brought you if you were. Now start using your noggin."

"Maybe I'm just a late bloomer in the panicking department?"

"Maybe it's your transition into squirreldom?" Beren suggested.

Okay, so I couldn't help smiling at that. "Maybe."

He smiled back. "That's better." He turned to Angelica. "So there's nothing there about the body."

"No."

"While you work out how we're getting out of here, I'm going to inspect our dead mate and see what I can find."

Angelica gave him a nod, then turned back to the puzzle in front of her. When she spoke, it was almost as if she were thinking out loud. "Hmm, we have more than one choice. We could attempt to absorb the force and send it outward when we get where we're going, but I don't like that because we might fail, and if we succeed, we have no idea where they're going to dump us. It could be somewhere surrounded by innocents."

"What's our other choice?" Imani asked.

"Create shields to deflect the explosion, but the power of what's set up could mean we arrive exhausted and unable to fight back. One or all of us could burn out. Both scenarios assume we won't just blow up because we haven't got enough power."

Great choices. I kept that in my brain because no one needed that negativity right now. As Imani had reminded me, that kind of thinking wouldn't help. How would positive Lily think about this? Hmm…. I put up my hand.

"Yes, dear?"

"This might but a stupid suggestion because I don't know much about how it all works." I swallowed the nervousness that told me everyone was going to laugh. No one would laugh —they weren't like that—but it was hard to overcome the knowledge that I really didn't know a quarter of what they all did when it came to constructing and deflecting spells. What I did was mainly think and hope. I hadn't delved into a full understanding of how it really worked. As far as I was concerned, magic was just a bunch of miracle-hocus-pocus stuff, like turning on the light was or flying in a plane. I accepted it happened, but if I had to create it from scratch, you can bet we'd be living in the dark ages, or at least in the trees with the squirrels.

"Spit it out, dear. We're listening."

"What if Will explodes all the video cameras hiding in this room, and I stand in the middle of you lot. You have your backs to me, so you're ready to see and act when we get where we're going. But you all reach behind and touch me with one hand—I could touch two of you on the shoulder—and you all channel your power through me. If we stand near the front door, one of you could stick your toe out to activate the explosion. Once we get where we're going, you'll all be ready with your guns or magic. I'll drop my connection to you once we're transported."

Angelica scratched her neck as she thought. James's forehead wrinkled, but his gaze was thoughtful. "That could actually work, and when we arrive wherever it is we're going, if we don't think we can beat them, you can throw a doorway up around all of us, sending us to headquarters."

Imani frowned. "That's one hell of a big doorway, love."

"She can do it."

"Even after channelling all that power to divert the explosion?" Imani was right to question James. I wasn't sure it would work, but I had to give them options if I could.

Angelica nodded slowly. "I believe that could work." She stared at me. "It's going to be taxing on you though, and no matter how much it hurts, you can't drop the power or cut off the source. Any backing out will kill us all, which is the only downside. If each of us were to protect ourselves, at least some of us would be able to withstand the blast... one would think."

There were those odds again. I swallowed the adrenaline-fuelled lump that rose in my throat. I could accidentally kill everyone. "Are you sure you want to volunteer for this? That's a lot of responsibility. We won't judge you if you decide you don't want to take that risk—because, make no mistake, no matter how powerful you are, you might still fail."

My chest expanded with a shuddering breath. "What are the chances of all of us surviving if we don't do it that way?"

Her steady gaze didn't do anything to calm my pounding heart. "All of us surviving, I'd say 20 per cent. If we do it your way, I'd say our chances increase to 40 per cent. But the chance of at least two of us surviving if it was every person for themselves would be closer to 50 per cent."

I looked at James. For Mum's sake, at least one of us had to survive. For my sake, I hoped it was James. He had Millicent and Annabelle. And then there was Will. If he died, I'd find it almost impossible to keep going. How could you be happy when the love of your life was gone? And Imani, my gorgeous friend. It would break my heart. Beren, Angelica, they were like family. I shut my eyes and rubbed my eyelids. *What should I do?*

Beren came into the room. "Oh, what did I miss?"

Angelica turned her head to look at him. "Did you find anything?"

"Yes. I can narrow down his time of death to within two hours of when Craft showed up at headquarters. Which doesn't solve anything right now."

Angelica nodded. "We need that body."

Will looked at her. "I can carry him."

"That's not practical, dear. He'll slow you down if we get into a fight."

He shrugged. "I'll use him as a shield." Oh, God, how

gruesome. But Will was so good with pets. You never really could tell what someone was like until you'd been in a life-and-death situation with them and you needed to drag a dead body along.

Determination firmed Will's posture. "We need him to close our case. This whole thing came about because they're trying to make us look like a useless bunch of amateurs. I won't let them win. If they want the PIB disbanded, they'll have to try harder than that. If we leave the body in this explosion, there'll be no trace he ever existed."

Except for my photos....

Damn having to keep this secret. All the things we could achieve if I could just be out in the open. Although, even if I were, we'd probably be accused of faking the photos or footage. What people achieved with computers these days was ridiculous. But there must be spells for checking authenticity.

"Lily?" James waved his hand in front of my face.

"Oh, ah, yes?"

His mouth kinked up on one side. "Always off with the squirrels. To be honest, I wouldn't mind hanging out with them right now, but since we're here, why don't we focus?" His kind tone took the sting out of his criticism.

"Sorry."

"I'll update you, dear. Will is going to carry our suspect. When you make our final doorway, you'll have to allow for that."

My eyes bugged wide. "You're going with my plan? Are you crazy?"

Angelica laughed. "Possibly. But after more thought, I do think you're our best option. Maybe our chances are slightly more than I originally estimated. You're the strongest one here, and with all our power combined, as long as you don't lose the plot in the middle of everything, we stand a good chance. But you must ignore any pain. Even if you feel like you're going to burn out, keep going."

What the hell? She'd never said that before. I put a hand on my stomach. I wouldn't necessarily die, but I would never be able to use my magic again. But Mum had suffered that, too, and so what? I'd be just like her again. And that was okay. Sacrificing my magic was a small price to pay to keep my loved ones safe because not having them would ruin my life, whether I still had magic or not. A lifetime of grieving would be ahead of me, no matter how many doorways I could step through. I might lose the ability to speak to the squirrels, but I could still feed them and sit with them. My life wouldn't be over—it would just be different. Normal.

I lifted my head, ready to take on the evil monsters who were trying to bring us down. No one tried to kill my family and got away with it—and make no mistake, everyone in this room was my family.

I returned Angelica's grave stare with one of my own. "I'm ready. Feel free to be a back-seat spellcaster if I do anything wrong."

"You'll do just fine, dear." She gave a firm nod. "It's best if you get inside yourself and follow your instincts. The less interruptions for you, the better."

I licked my lips. Crap was about to get real.

Will's magic tickled my scalp, and four small pops sounded as video cameras exploded. "Done. No one can see us now." He smiled. "I'll be back in a sec." He hurried off to get Larsen. At least the guy wasn't huge. He was shorter and less built than Will. When he returned with the body slung over his shoulder, we all made our way toward the front door.

Angelica stopped a few feet from the open door. The car

we'd borrowed wasn't going to be taken home. I guessed emergency services would find it when the house blew. Hopefully, the car wouldn't go up with it. I hoped that car was insured. If we survived, I'd get Angelica to check what happened to the car. Maybe the PIB could reimburse the owners.

"Lily?" Angelica stared at me, the wrinkles in her forehead shattering her calm mask. "You must concentrate. Have I made the wrong call? Tell me now if I have."

"Sorry. I was just worried about the car. I promise I'll focus. Once I'm drawing my magic, I'll be fine. I guess I'm nervous."

"Okay." She blew out a big breath. "Does everyone have their return to senders up?" We all nodded. Angelica trained her gaze on me again. "Don't make a doorway unless I say the word. And everyone else, be ready to travel when that happens. Don't make any sudden movements if you can help it."

"What word am I listening for?"

She smiled. "Squirrel." I smiled and gave her a thumbs up. Funny how, even in great turmoil, the thought of my furry little friends could cheer me up.

Angelica had one more thing to tell me. "When you imagine the shield, imagine it clear and thick, like bulletproof glass. Imagine it keeping us safe and repelling anything that could possibly come at it. These explosions are usually magically intensified so the impact and heat last longer. They're going to do their best to break through our defences."

I rolled my shoulders back and stood straight. "But they have no idea how strong we are."

Imani smiled. "How strong you are, love. Let's do this."

We stood in a circle, me in the middle, everyone else facing outwards, guns drawn. Will was closest to the door, ready to hold Larsen's foot out. I guessed he wouldn't be needing that foot anyway. My shield was going to cut it off.

I stood with my arms parallel to the floor, creating a straight line. I put a hand on Will's shoulder and one on Angelica's. James stepped backwards until my front was touching his back. Imani and Beren stood back to back with me, our shoulder blades touching. I was safe in a cocoon of brave-agent bodies.

Now it was my turn to protect them.

I opened myself up to the power. "Can everyone open to the river?"

They did as asked.

"Tell me when, Lily." For all the weight he was carrying, Will's voice was steady and strong.

"I'll let you know by saying 'now.'"

"Okay."

I shut my eyes and sucked in as much power as I could hold, ready for more to flood through when we were linked. This was going to hurt; it was going to exhaust me, but I couldn't let go.

I couldn't fail.

Too much was riding on this.

The beat of my blood thudding past my ears became my war song.

I breathed through my nose, as if I were going for a run— in, one two three, out, one two three. This was going to get tough. I silently asked my magic to create a bullet- and explosion-proof barrier. I imagined it thick, secure, impenetrable. When I was sure it was as strong as I could make it by myself, I said, "Send me your power."

I shut my eyes. My head fell back as the surge hit.

Someone gasped. It was as if sound was coming at me

through a closed doorway. I sensed no danger... yet. No matter what happened, I needed to see this through. I set aside the distraction.

I spoke to my magic but loud enough that Will heard so he knew what I planned. "When Will flicks the dead guy's foot out, let it out and shut the shield on it."

I sensed the thickness of the shield, fed more power into it. Fortified it.

Sweat tickled my temples. My body prickled with heat. I concentrated on holding it all together and took a deep breath.

Five.

Four.

Three.

Two.

One.

"Now!"

I had no idea how the shield would react to that foot coming out. Even though I'd said what I wanted, I didn't know the law of shields. Fingers crossed it would let the appendage out and close before the explosion detonated.

The breach in the shield was like the nudge of an elbow to my side. Within a moment, the sensation smoothed as the invisible barrier sealed. The foot was cast. I had only a fraction of a second of relief before all hell broke loose.

It was as if my shield was being sucked away from me. I held tight, keeping it close to our circle. A high-pitched whistle drilled into my eardrums, but I couldn't protect my ears.

Must keep hands on Will and Angelica.

Silence.

Boom! A sword of sharp pain sliced through my ears. Bright light flashed through my closed eyelids. The floor shook, jostling us. If we lost contact, the shield would lose power.

"Stay with me!" I shouted over the cacophony.

A tornado of fierce heat buffeted the shield. I gritted my teeth. What had been a distant heat burrowed into my shield. The stabbing of something metallic and sharp into it near James's heart sent shooting pain through my stomach. My eyes were closed, but I could sense the position of every burn and strike.

I was one with the shield.

I was the shield.

I sucked in more power through my friends until my blood burned as hot as my armour. Pushing more magic into the part of the shield protecting James's heart, my stomach constricted, cramps hitting me in waves.

Still the fire raged, and projectiles assaulted the barrier.

I staggered to one side, almost losing my grip on Angelica. My breath came in pants. Not enough oxygen. Sweat poured off my face. Hot.

Everything was so hot.

My feet wanted to run. I planted them more firmly. *Stay.* A solid, heavy object slammed into the shield. I grunted and gasped for air, the force of the strike winding me. Smoke, thick, acidic soured my nostrils.

I took more power. Imani's laboured breaths reached my ears, and James muttered something. I gritted my teeth. "Hold on."

I didn't know how much longer we could sustain this, but I wanted it to end. James's weight against my front increased as he leaned into me.

My veins blistered. I was on the verge of being cremated from the inside out. It didn't matter. I drew more and more energy from the river and my friends, asked for it all, a dam of fire ready to spill over.

My cry, when it came, grazed my throat. I threw my shield outwards, needing to end this inferno once and for all. "Argh!" A great rush of noise, a whoosh that took all other sound and snatched it away, thrashed around us and past.

Leaving silence.

Everything shifted.

Dizziness struck, and I fell to my knees, my hands trailing along Will's and Angelica's backs—I didn't want to lose contact. My hands found their ankles and held tight. James, bereft of my support, fell with me. I opened my eyes, surprised I hadn't left a trail of fire down Will's and Angelica's backs. James had reached out to me with one hand when I'd started falling. He never lost contact and now squatted, his fingers finding my leg and gripping tightly. He kept his gaze on what was happening out there in the blackness.

I sucked in breath after breath, hating the sensation of my damp clothes clinging to my sweat-drenched body but loving that we were still alive… for now.

The darkness stretched into grey before a ray of light pierced the gloom. It grew wider as the sensation of speeding through a tunnel gripped me. With light surrounding us, we free fell a couple of feet and hit hard. Jagged pain sawed through my knees. Will swore. James let out a small groan.

Angelica said, "Everyone, check in."

We answered yes, one by one around the circle, starting with Beren. When we finished, a room coalesced around us. I checked my return to sender. It was, shockingly, still up. I still had some fight left in me, thank God.

We'd been spat out on a concrete floor in an industrial factory unit, its high roofline supported by metal beams.

Under those beams stood five men—one of them was the humungous man in my photos who'd transported our suspect to the house. He seemed even larger in real life, especially since I was on the floor.

The men's eyes bugged wide, and a couple had mouths hanging open, a cigarette falling from one mouth. I ignored the throbbing in my knees and scrambled to my feet. Will, who was already standing, threw the body on the floor. Oh, crap. We were going to do this.

I whispered to Angelica, "Doorway or not?" Optimism had me readying my magic to make the sizable doorway we'd need.

"No. This ends here." Damn, why'd she have to say that?

"Cool." *Not cool.* Surely everyone was exhausted. I'd pushed everyone hard, like a sadistic personal trainer. I had some energy left, but how much, I didn't know.

Will took advantage of their shock—they'd obviously expected dead bodies to come through. We only had one, and it wasn't the one they wanted dead. Will pointed at the man closest to him and shot. It was straight to the heart. The man looked down at his chest in surprise before falling forward. I cringed at the crack as his head hit the floor.

As James and Angelica took aim at two of the other men, unfamiliar magic prickled my scalp, and a shield shimmered in front of the remaining men. I would've thrown up a barrier, but I didn't have it in me. Our return to senders were all we had left.

Now what?

Beren had moved around to stand next to Angelica. I sensed they both held magic. When I looked more closely, I saw they'd each thrown an invisible protection around themselves. I was inside Beren's, and Angelica's took in James. Will finally protected himself, as did Imani.

Who was stronger? Them—fresh from doing nothing—or us—having just survived the almost unsurvivable?

The big guy flexed his guns and grinned, showing off his tar-stained array of mangled teeth. *Noice.* He then reached behind himself and picked up a machine gun off a work-bench. Crap.

The singlet-wearing criminal next to him, tatts covering every inch of visible skin except his face, glowed vibrantly with magic. He was strong. I poked Angelica in the back. "Doorway?"

She gave them all the once over, then, without taking her gaze off the men, whispered, "Pick him up. We'll cover you; then we're gone."

Will bent and reached down.

One of the men dropped his shield and pointed his gun at Will. Magic shot through me from the river, and I screamed as I threw my fear and hate at him. Lightning cracked and knifed down from above, cleaving through his body and blackening the floor.

Imani spared me a glance. "Overkill much?"

Will had Larsen's body safely in his grasp. I wasn't wasting any time. "One doorway coming right up."

I drew my power one last time and imagined a huge doorway that would safely encompass all of us, sending us to the PIB. Exhaustion hit me as the workshop and seething men disappeared. As soon as we stood in the reception room, I fell into a chair. The headache had started, and I battled to keep my eyes open. But we would live to fight another day, which I was grateful for. The only problem was, I was so sick of fighting.

When would the war end? Unfortunately, the answer to that was one I didn't want to think about. If I had enough power, I'd magic all the bad witches out of existence. Except I wasn't strong enough. Damn it.

Gus opened the reception-room door and held it wide—someone must have buzzed, but I hadn't noticed. "Good evening, Ma'am, all."

"Good evening, Gus." Angelica was the first person to exit, her hair in disarray. That's how fatigued she was. It was nice to see she wasn't always perfect. As everyone else filed out, Will carrying our prize, James waited for me.

"Come on, sis. Good job, by the way."

I gave him a tired smile. "Thanks. You all did okay too."

"Thanks." He held out a hand to help me up. I took it and stood, my knees almost giving way. I rolled my eyes. Stupid legs. You'd think they'd be used to this by now. "Why don't you go home? I'm sure we can manage without you for tonight."

"Are you sure?"

He smiled. "Positive."

"Thanks. Say hi to Mum for me." I gave him a hug because we'd almost died… again… plus, why not?

"Will do." He released me. "Do you want me to make the doorway?" The skin beneath his eyes was shadowed, and he had more to do today.

"No. I can manage. I'll go straight to bed."

He gave a wave, then walked through the reception-room door, letting it close behind him. I made my doorway and stepped through to Angelica's reception room. Then I trudged up the stairs, got changed the normal way, and slid into bed for a long sleep.

Not once did I feel regret about the man I'd killed. Guilt

walked right on past without even tapping on my door. I knew that should worry me, but I didn't have the energy to care.

My transformation into a cold-blooded killer was almost complete.

But it was for the good of the world… wasn't it?

I honestly wasn't sure, but for the sake of sleep tonight, that's what I told myself. Maybe I'd repent in the morning.

Or maybe I wouldn't.

Maybe I was too far gone.

CHAPTER 10

I slept through the night. Will, the kind soul that he was, snuck into bed without waking me, and we came to with the 8:00 a.m. alarm. Abby had slept in between us all night and Ted on his doggy bed on the floor at the end of our bed. Waking surrounded by all the cuteness—the pets—and handsomeness—Will—made me smile. I'd enjoy my contentment today—there was time to feel guilty later. Although, maybe I never would feel it. I wished I could just remember these people were out to kill us, so they deserved no sympathy. I vowed to save the guilt for things that deserved it.

Will yawned. "Morning, mistress of the magic."

I rubbed one eye and snuggled in for a cuddle. "That's a lofty title."

"For lofty achievements. You really saved us yesterday."

"I'm sure you would've survived without me."

He ran a caring hand over my head and along my shoulder. "No. We all talked about it last night." He gently nudged me off him and turned to lie on his side and elbow, his head propped up by his hand. "Without us linking and joining forces, that spell would've overpowered us. More than one person fed that spell, Lily. We're not sure how they did it, but there was enough magic flying at us that I wouldn't be surprised if a full circle of witches was involved."

My heart raced, and my face flushed. Crap. We'd come so close. I hadn't realised. Jesus, what if I'd made a mistake? What if we hadn't had enough power to fight it? What if I'd burnt out before we'd won?

Will rested his forehead on mine. "Stop thinking. I can see the panic on your face. There's no point catastrophising now. We did it. We escaped."

"But we almost didn't. I was hanging on by my fingernails."

"You might be surprised, Lily. That decision you made, to push into the spell rather than just defend, that's what did it. And I don't think you realise the amount of power and strength it takes to do it, even with all of us backing you up. Just channelling that amount of magic… well… it's ridiculous what you're capable of."

I couldn't help but succumb to the pride warming my stomach—it was a hell of a lot better than the heat that came with drawing too much power, that was for sure. "Thanks. But it's not something I earned. I was born with it. I can hardly claim awesomeness when all I have to do is hold on."

"Born with it or not, it takes fortitude of mind and a high pain threshold, oh, and don't forget the bravery—you must've known you were skirting the edge of losing your power or dying."

"Ah, yes, thanks for the reminder." I gave him a wry smile. "It had crossed my mind, but we would've died anyway at that point. There wasn't a choice as far as I could tell." And there wasn't. Any witch would have done the same in that situation; I was sure of it.

"It does leave us with a problem."

"Seriously? Why does there have to be repercussions for surviving? Sheesh."

He smiled. "Yeah, I know. Anyway, the issue is that they don't know which one of us defeated their power, but they know we were joined—there's no other way we could've survived it otherwise. And since there wasn't the requisite number of witches for the joining, they know one of us has special talents."

"Or an amulet."

"True. The upshot is that even though they'll be warier of us now, they'll be even more eager to squash us as soon as possible."

"Do you mean the directors or the criminals?"

His pause was just a bit too long. I had time to figure out what his answer was and hate it before it even came out of his mouth. "Both."

Someone knocked on the door. Three polite raps. "Come in," I called out.

The door opened. Angelica's face popped around, and when she'd ascertained we were decent, she opened the door wider. She and Mum came in and stood just inside the door. "Morning." Mum's smile was wide, even though her eyes spoke of distress.

I smiled back. "Morning. Sorry I didn't call you when I got back. I was too tired."

She waved the comment away. "It's fine. James told me everything. I was so worried after we got off the phone." She held a hand up to her décolletage. "I'm just so relieved you're okay. If you weren't in bed with your hunky man, I'd give you a hug." Angelica smirked.

I groaned. "Hunky? Really?"

Will grinned and gave me a "see" look. "I agree, Kat. I am hunky. Thanks for noticing."

I laughed. "You're such a dag." I looked up at Mum. "And so are you."

Angelica's smile slid from her face. "Sorry to do this now, but we have work to do, and everyone else has been updated. I need to impart this information, then get on with my day."

"Oh, what is it?" I sat up, my T-shirt decent enough for this company, even if I wasn't wearing a bra underneath. Abby shifted, stood, glared at me for disturbing her, then hopped off the bed. She made sure her tail was lifted in the air as she sauntered out, revealing her displeasure. Typical cat.

Angelica came further into the room and leaned against my study table. "First of all, I want to say thank you for yesterday. We've come away with the criminal and our lives. That's as successful a mission as we could ever hope for." I opened my mouth to say no probs, but she held up her hand. "Unfortunately…" Gah, not another caveat. Why couldn't things just be nice and easy? "While the directors aren't ready to come right out and declare war, I've received an email from the funding review board, and they've put us on notice."

That was her bad news? It didn't seem so bad compared to what it could've been. "That doesn't sound that bad, unless they're not impartial."

Mum and Angelica shared a look. Mum said, "We haven't confirmed that yet, but we have to assume they have at least one supporter on the board—bribery gets you places, and if that fails, blackmail works even better."

"Anyway, dear, that's not the worst of it." Whyyyyyyyyy? "That man you zapped."

I sat forward, and my voice raised involuntarily. "You mean the one who was about to kill my fiancé?"

"Yes, dear, that one. He happens to be the brother of the head of one of the criminal syndicates supporting the directors." Ah, crap. Even I knew that wasn't good.

There was always a price to pay for impulsiveness. But could I be anything other than impulsive when someone was going to kill the man I loved? There was no time to plan. We were living in a reality where it was kill or be killed. How the hell had I gotten here?

"Or forcing the directors' hands." My mother was always the optimist, but I didn't think she was that naïve. Maybe she was playing devil's advocate?

Angelica's sour face left no guesses as to how she felt about that. "In any case, there are now prices on all our heads, but yours is for the most money because you killed a powerful criminal leader's brother."

Will sat up, too, exposing his gorgeous chest. He really was hunky. Shame I had more pressing things to think about right now. "How much?"

Angelica's gaze slid from Will to me and back to Will. "Two million pounds."

"Crap."

Will swore… repeatedly.

"I know, William. I know." Angelica folded her arms. "You two, take it easy today, but take it easy inside. I don't want you going anywhere until we formulate a plan. Millicent's father is also going to come over and make sure our protection spells are up to date."

We knew this was coming, one way or another, so I wasn't

going to bother getting upset about yet another home deten-tion. "What about Chadiot? Are you going to cut him loose now?"

"No. He could still come in handy, and we don't need him running around causing more trouble. We have enough as it is."

Will nodded at Angelica. "I couldn't agree more."

Angelica looked at my mother. "Come on, Kat. We have lots of work to do."

We said goodbye, and they left, shutting the door behind them. I looked at Will. "Why didn't you ask how much was on your head?"

"Because they have the biggest price on yours. Not being as valuable as you has dented my ego as it is. I don't need to find out they only think I'm worth five hundred quid." He smirked, but the fun didn't reach his eyes.

I swallowed and stared at the wall, not ready for another survival roller coaster. I wasn't much into carnival rides, espe-cially not ones that ended in death.

Will caressed my cheek with a finger. "Oh, I forgot to thank you for saving me."

I slid my gaze to his. "You never have to thank me for that. If you died, you'd take my heart with you."

"Well, even though you don't want me to thank you, I will. It's not like we have anything else to do today." He grinned, and this time I felt it all the way to my toes.

I'd treat today as a time out. Tomorrow would come soon enough. "Okay, then. If you insist."

"I do."

"So, what are you waiting for, hunky?" I waggled my eyebrows.

He gave me a fake shocked face. "You're going to pay for that."

"Promise?" I grinned. Even with a price on my head, Will made me feel like the luckiest woman alive.

But that's probably because I was.

❦

If you've enjoyed story, book 18, *Witch Karma in Westerham*, is out now or might enjoy my new cosy mystery series, Haunting Avery Winters. Book 1—A Killer Welcome.

Avery Winters was overjoyed to be brought back to life... unfortunately, the dead were waiting for her.

Aussie journalist Avery Winters was content—she had a caring boyfriend, great job, and supportive... okay, so her parents weren't actually supportive, but she'd accepted she could never be the son they'd wanted seeing as how she was born a girl. Avoiding them seemed to work well, and, she reasoned, no one's life was perfect.

And that was fine, except whilst covering a news story in a storm, Avery's cosy life disappeared in a flash. Lightning struck, stopping her heart and blowing her favourite black boots to smithereens. It was pure luck that an off-duty nurse was walking nearby.

When Avery came to in the ambulance en route to hospital, she'd thought the worst was over. She was wrong.

Her lightning-induced hallucinations—there was no way they were ghosts—were impossible to hide. Her boyfriend soon left, and her boss suggested she take extended leave. Unable to cover her rent, she moved back in with her parents. And that's when the fun really began. Unable to cope with their insistence she was crazy, and desperate for an escape, she responded to a journalist-wanted ad… in the UK, because getting mega far away from her parents could only be a good thing.

Armed with a new fear of storms, companions others couldn't see, and the hope that leaving the stress behind would improve her mental state, she boarded a plane for London. What she didn't count on was not being able to leave her ghosts behind… literally. Oh, and that the quaint English village she'd be living in had more skeletons in its closet than the Natural History Museum.

When she stumbles upon a dead body in her rented apartment on her first day, she's tempted to get back on the plane. But whilst it's not a good omen, returning to her parents would be worse, so she decides to stay. Only, she's not sure if it's the best decision she's ever made, or the worst.

She's about to find out.

ALSO BY DIONNE LISTER

Paranormal Investigation Bureau

Witchnapped in Westerham #1

Witch Swindled in Westerham #2

Witch Undercover in Westerham #3

Witchslapped in Westerham #4

Witch Silenced in Westerham #5

Killer Witch in Westerham #6

Witch Haunted in Westerham #7

Witch Oracle in Westerham #8

Witchbotched in Westerham #9

Witch Cursed in Westerham #10

Witch Heist in Westerham #11

Witch Burglar in Westerham #12

Vampire Witch in Westerham #13

Witch War in Westerham #14

Westerham Witches and a Venetian Vendetta #15

Witch Nemesis in Westerham #16

Witch Catastrophe in Westerham #17

Witch Karma in Westerham Book #18

Witch Showdown in Westerham #19

Westerham Witches and an Aussie Misadventure #20

Haunting Avery Winters

(Paranormal Cosy Mystery)

A Killer Welcome #1

A Regrettable Roast #2

A Fallow Grave #3

A Frozen Stiff #4

A Deadly Drive-by #5

A Caffeine Hit #6

The Circle of Talia

(YA Epic Fantasy)

Shadows of the Realm

A Time of Darkness

Realm of Blood and Fire

The Rose of Nerine

(Epic Fantasy)

Tempering the Rose

Forging The Rose

ABOUT THE AUTHOR

USA Today bestselling author, Dionne Lister is a Sydneysider with a degree in creative writing and two Siamese cats. Daydreaming has always been her passion, so writing was a natural progression from staring out the window in primary school, and being an author was a dream she held since childhood.

Unfortunately, writing was only a hobby while Dionne worked as a property valuer in Sydney, until her mid-thirties when she returned to study and completed her creative writing degree. Since then, she has indulged her passion for writing while raising two children with her husband. Her books have attracted praise from Apple iBooks and have reached #1 on Amazon and iBooks charts worldwide, frequently occupying top 100 lists in fantasy and mystery.